THUG #1

JAMES WYMORE
JOHN CHRISTIAN PERKINS

Appropriate for Teens, Intriguing to Adults

Immortal Works LLC
1505 Glenrose Drive
Salt Lake City, Utah 84104
Tel: (385) 202-0116

Cover Art & Illustrations by John Christian Perkins
www.drawformeJCP.com

Interior Formatting by FireDrake Designs
www.firedrakedesigns.com

ISBN 978-1-7324674-7-7 (paperback)
AISN: B07MXCZ94M (Kindle edition)

For the Originals:
Jason and Holli

1

CJ Cruz had a chain wrapped around a man's neck from behind. When Mad-Mikey slugged that man in the stomach, the breath went out of him and he went down on his knees. CJ put one knee behind his neck and held him in place while he sucked in breath and choked. The smooth metal of the chain pinched in a few places where he held it.

They were in an alley, but the opening to the west gave them plenty of afternoon light. A few men and women, all working with CJ for Doctor Pain these days, surrounded the well-built man in his early thirties.

"I'm going to ask you one more time. Where's Snake-man?" Mad-Mikey recently ascended to become Doctor Pain's right hand man. He made sure everybody in the Denver underground knew about it, too. He'd personally chosen everyone in the group. CJ had no illusions about being picked because he was tougher than anybody else in Doctor Pain's gang. Mad-Mikey knew CJ wasn't interested in taking over as the boss's top dog, so he trusted CJ, after a fashion.

CJ loosened the chain so the man could speak, and breathe better. "I told you, I don't know." The man had a sports jacket over a silk shirt. He worked as a bouncer at the bar they were behind. They'd ambushed him on his way to work before the place even opened. Nothing said class like fighting six to one.

Mad-Mikey shook his head. "He was in here last night, shaking down some of Doctor Pain's crew. Word around town is, he comes here a lot. So spill it, or I'll have CJ here finish you off as a message to the scaly coward."

CJ winced. *Thou shalt not kill.* He wouldn't do it. He wasn't getting paid nearly enough for that much heat, in jail or hell. In fact, he didn't really appreciate Mad-Mikey using his name. Cops tended to follow up on solid leads, and he already had a record.

The bouncer shook his head. "He doesn't talk to me, he just…"

Pointing violently, Mikey yelled, "Where does he go?"

The man tipped his head to look up as one eye began to swell. "Sometimes when I call him a cab he asks to go to Lakewood. That's all I know, man. If you let me go, I promise I won't tell him anything."

Mad-Mikey turned his head sideways and squinted with one eye, overdoing the crazy angle, CJ thought. He pointed straight at the bouncer's good

eye. "No, you will tell him. I want you to tell him Doctor Pain is coming and we won't stop until he's dead."

CJ let the chain go slack and stepped away. Mikey glared. CJ put his hands out and shrugged.

Mikey waved for the group to take off. "You tell him we're coming."

The man wisely stayed on his knees as the group followed the number-one goon out into the street. CJ pulled his Broncos cap down lower and walked toward the back. He'd thought Mikey was done with the guy. He wasn't a mind reader. Things would have gone very different if he could read the man's thoughts. He wouldn't be wasting his power chasing down nobodies in back alleys, to begin with. No point thinking that way; he wasn't a Super. He just got paid to work for them.

His mom wouldn't have seen it that way, bless her soul. Still, he felt a pang of guilt as he dropped the chain into his large pocket. He signed on to fight Supers, not beat up normal, working class people.

Later that evening, CJ sat at a table among a troop of hired muscle. Most of them were indulging in the plentiful free drinks. CJ sipped at a water on the rocks. Doctor Pain stood at the end of the restaurant's conference room. His thick gold necklace glinted in the dim light against his dark skinned chest. His eyes sparkled beneath black, buzz-cut hair. Steroid enhanced muscles bulged out of his pharmacist jacket with torn off sleeves.

Doctor Pain brought his fist down on one of the wooden tables in the room. "Snake-man has been getting in the way for too long. Yesterday he took out three of our own. It's time somebody took him down. With your help, I'm that somebody."

The crowd cheered a low approval.

Despite the name, CJ doubted this guy had a Ph.D. Even worse, he was beginning to think Doctor Pain didn't even have a legitimate Super power. The criterion for what made somebody "Super" was kind of a gray area. A body builder with a bit of charm could take on a pseudonym and hire a gang of thugs, but that didn't make him a Super. Unfortunately, in Denver, for a guy in CJ's line of work, Doctor Pain was the only game in town.

"Who here has been injured or slighted by Snake-man?" Doctor Pain scanned the crowd with his dark, piercing eyes. Mad-Mikey stood behind their leader with his hands behind his back, trying to keep one eye half-closed and still look tough.

"I haven't had a decent meal since he came to town," Eduardo called from across the room.

"I fancy some barbecued snake meat!" yelled Steven. CJ knew most, if not all, of the thirty plus gathered henchmen. Except the noobs, he'd worked with them in various capacities over the years. A lot of them hadn't yet figured out how things really worked in this business. They still thought loyalty and passion led to success. He wouldn't bother trying to set them straight. They'd figure it out if they lasted long enough.

"My sources have found where the slithering idiot lives. Tonight, we take him out. Tomorrow, we take over the city!"

More cheering. Men and women dressed in an eclectic mix of everything from cowboy boots to Kevlar began pounding their glasses on the table and hollering. CJ put his chin up and smiled to show support to anybody who made eye contact. So somebody else had found their quarry. Mikey would be working double time to justify his position.

Even if they took out the resident defender, this group wouldn't hold out long. They weren't even as organized as most street gangs. That didn't matter. All CJ needed was for them to fill the power void long enough for him to get a paycheck.

It was always hit and miss in this game. Most of the Supers interested in hiring help had specific tastes, bordering on fetishism. One guy wanted everybody dressed like birds, another Super would only hire women. Luckily, Doctor Pain was just looking for brute force. CJ could do that. Still, the more cerebral Supers, looking for specific skill sets, were better employers. They tended to last longer, too.

CJ texted his daughter. *I'm stuck at my new job. Raincheck for dinner tonight?*

Juliet responded quickly, never far from her phone. *Good. Mom says if you don't come up with some money soon she's cutting your visitation... and if I don't get some time out of the house I'll go crazy.*

CJ shook his head. They'd been divorced for years, and he'd mostly been up on his child support. Would it kill her to cut him some slack once in a while? He wrote, *That's the up side to a new job, I won't have to come visit you in the asylum.*

A few seconds later, she answered. *I thought they banned you because all your old bosses were in there. ;)*

"Pfft!" CJ laughed and spit some of his water out on the table. When the men at his table scowled, he put his hands up and mumbled, "Sorry." Steven grabbed a napkin to wipe the spray off his tattooed arm. CJ typed, *Only half. Jury's still out on the newest one.*

Be safe. She was smarter than everybody in this room put together.

"First we eat, then we hunt the snake!" Doctor Pain had his hands up like he'd just scored the winning touchdown. Servers began bringing in pizza and breadsticks.

CJ texted his girlfriend, Delia. *Good prospects on the new opportunity.*

She didn't respond. That meant she was probably working a late shift to cover for somebody who didn't show up.

Even though he was hungry, CJ tipped his Broncos baseball cap to Sasha, who was sitting next to him, and stood up.

She said, "Where you going?"

"Get some air. I want to take a look around. I don't like being stuck in a crowded room too long. You want to help?"

She tipped her porkpie hat back and half closed one eye, "And miss the pizza?"

CJ smiled. "Save me a slice."

She laughed. "In this room, you'll be lucky if the food lasts two minutes."

He grabbed a couple breadsticks off one of the serving platters as he went out the front door. "Big crowd," he said to the waitress.

"Not big tippers, though." She bit her lip and looked down.

CJ laughed. "I thought Doctor Pain was rolling in dough."

"Maybe, but I won't see a dime of it." She lowered the tray as a dozen hands descended like vultures. "Can't afford to lose this job, and I don't think this building could handle two Super powers going at it if the Snake shows up."

CJ looked at Doctor Pain again. "Well, maybe one and a half."

"What?" She paused, her tray empty, and looked at his face.

He smiled and pushed the door open. Half a dozen people who should have been in the 'meeting' were outside chain-smoking or talking on their phones.

He dropped the good-natured act when he rounded the corner. Something wasn't right. All his instincts told him this was a bad idea. He needed the work, so he would stick it out. Still, he wanted to get his bearings, apart from the raucous group.

Out in the cool night air, he realized the problem. There were too many of them in too public a place. Doctor Pain was a nobody in the Super world. He didn't have the clout to keep this information under wraps. Nobody knew him well enough to fear retribution. He hadn't even beaten Snake-man in a fight yet.

CJ's stomach twisted into a knot. He took a deep breath and jogged across the parking area. He went up a berm of earth where a few bushes and trees grew between the lot and the street. He waited there and chewed on the breadsticks. If nothing went wrong, he could always join the crowd as they stormed Snake-man's house and nobody would be the wiser.

A group of teens, dressed in baggy clothes and backward hats, strutted up, making plenty of noise.

"You know Doctor Pain?" a boy shorter than five feet tall asked with a forced accent.

CJ tipped his head to the pizza place. "He's inside. Why?"

"We were invited to join his crew," said a larger boy with a gold tooth.

"Might want to hold off on that a bit," CJ said. These kids needed direction, not a job with a Supervillain, or just a regular villain, or whatever.

"Forget that noise," said the short one. "We're ready to take over." They knuckle-bumped each other and continued sauntering toward the restaurant.

CJ rolled his eyes. "Hey, wait."

They stopped and Gold Tooth gestured with his fingers. "We ain't got time for your nonsense."

"Have you paid your dues?" He stepped up to them, pulling the chain out of his pocket. "I'm the front man. Nobody goes in until they pay their dues."

"What?" The short one looked at the others and gave CJ the stink eye. "What's that noise?"

"You want in on the action, you gotta buy in. Everybody inside paid half a bill to be in on the take." He stared Gold Tooth in the face. "You want some of the territory, you invest up front."

The teens looked at each other. Gold Tooth said, "Two-fifty? How much territory does that get?"

CJ sighed. *Thou shalt not steal.* He'd half hoped his ruse would turn them off the idea, maybe save them another tagline on their juvie records. Was it really stealing if they gave him the money? Besides, they'd probably just use it on drugs and guns anyway. "Couple square miles. You can pick the turf if you fight well."

They all shrugged and shuffled their feet. Gold Tooth pulled a wad of bills out. "Everybody, give it up."

"I ain't got no fifty bucks," the short one said.

"Pay what you got, I'll cover the rest." Gold Tooth collected money from the others and counted his own out on top. Then he slapped it into CJ's hand with an attitude. "Now show us where to go."

"Right through the door." CJ jammed the wad into his pocket as the gang sauntered forward like they'd already proven their strength. Doctor Pain hadn't paid him yet, so this was fair tender for services rendered.

Several cars drove up from different directions. None of them had their lights on. They were all black and white.

Why hadn't he grabbed a slice of pizza on the way out?

2

Three days later, CJ stood outside the Guardian Angels Church watching women with colorful oven mitts carry pans of potluck food into the square brick building. He preferred a more gothic church, personally, but he couldn't turn down an invitation for a multi-parish mixer. The scent of au-gratin potatoes floated by him on the breeze. Normally, he preferred to skip the social side of church, but Delia had another swing shift at the bail bonds shop and he didn't have two quarters to rub together.

He tipped his cap back, and unzipped his hoodie to expose his only clean t-shirt. It was nice of the Father to invite him tonight, even if the priest treated him like he still needed converting. CJ shook his head, reluctant to give in so easily to the hunger eating holes into the walls of his stomach. Thirty-eight years old and he still didn't have a steady cash flow.

An explosion behind him shot trails of yellow firework sparks into the air. CJ spun on his worn basketball shoes, gray eyes wide-open as the small petals of the fire-flower slowly dropped and went dark. The sunset blazed orange across the random clouds behind the train docks.

CJ felt more than curiosity. It hadn't been a car crash or gas leak.

Another blast. This time, two red columns of fire rose into the air. De-

spite his hunger, CJ smelled something much more enticing than food. CJ sensed a job brewing.

As he darted along Fifty-Second Avenue, his lungs burned more than they used to. He was in decent shape for his age, but a hard sprint still took it out of him. As he approached, he saw a gray-haired old man huddling next to a wall, apparently scared by the lights and noise.

"Are you going to the pot-luck dinner?" CJ asked with a smile. He made sure none of his business associates were watching.

"You should get out of the line of fire," the man said. His wide eyes hinted at a mix of dementia and post-traumatic stress. "In war, people die if they aren't behind cover."

CJ lifted his hoodie up on one side like a bird wing and held it protectively over the man's head. "I'll keep you safe." They walked together back toward the church. CJ made sure the vet was in before he sprinted back toward the ruckus, tracking another burst of purple light. What did it say about him that he would rather risk his life chasing Supers than talk to old ladies about canning preserves?

With Doctor Pain and company all in jail, CJ had better than usual odds of getting hired. Still, he'd spent too much time around Supers to walk right out into their business. He left the parking circle at the end of the street and crouched behind a stack of long metal cylinders where he could see from relative safety. A man in a black top hat and metallic purple cloak put his hands in the air holding up a black wand with a white tip. One second later, a white light, brighter than a welding arc, lit up the surrounding buildings and trains.

A low moan preceded a man calling out, "I don't have to see you to destroy you, you little waste of human life."

CJ pulled his black hood up over his hat and zipped it. He rubbed the two moles on his left cheek as he followed the voice to a second figure emerging from behind one of the parked train cars. This larger man had a scaly green cape with a matching bodysuit that turned yellowish white along the belly. As if the costume weren't enough, a pine green 'S' logo emblazoned his chest. Snake-man. CJ didn't know the other Super, but he automatically favored anybody taking down the serpent who usually worked solo.

The reptilian man turned and spat at the purple clad dandy.

Two lines of thick venom squirted across the twenty feet separating the

two men. The man in the suit twisted, revealing playing cards tucked into the band of the hat. A purple bowtie and cummerbund rounded off the outfit.

Powerful acid smoked wherever it hit the shiny cape. The magician yanked the cape off, and tossed away the smoking pile of blackening fabric.

Snake-man stepped to the side as his vision recovered from the bright light. The magician held both hands up again.

Green fireworks exploded from his wand. His opponent jumped behind

the edge of the metal car, avoiding most of the sparks as small black dots of ash peppered the rusty metal siding.

The magician maneuvered to get a new line of sight.

As soon as he cleared the side of the train, two more jets of poison shot out from the shadow. CJ expected the magician to burn, but the vile goo went straight through him, steaming on the rocks and rails of the train tracks behind.

"What? How'd you do that?" asked Snake-man as he glanced around the corner.

"A Magician never reveals his tricks." The illusion disappeared, revealing the black tuxedo a few feet to the side.

"Whatever," the snake said. "How about we see if you can escape from a coffin?"

"Child's play. You know the best way to deal with a snake?"

The reptile suit blurred as the Super lunged to attack. The magician ducked, leaving his hat in the hands of the enemy as he disappeared. The confused snake turned the hat to look at the cards. "Two pair, aces and kings over a jack. That's not even a great hand."

"Jakak. It's my name. Jakak the Magnificent." The voice echoed from one of the many train cars.

Snake-man turned, disoriented. He flipped the hat over in his hands absently. A small brown-furred mammal flew up from the opening and latched with four clawed hands onto his face.

"Yow!" Crying out in pain and shock, the large Super tossed the hat and began swatting at the mongoose as it scratched and ripped at his face and hair. He finally managed to get a hand around it and threw the flailing mammal over the closest boxcar. The animal twisted and flipped as it disappeared.

CJ laughed silently behind one hand. The magician had style. Taking advantage of the distraction, CJ ran across the yard to skulk in the shadow of the closest train. He wished he'd brought his chain.

When Supers clashed, most people stayed far away. Half of Globeville must've seen these fireworks, but nobody else tried to get closer to the action. From his new position, he heard the occasional trucks speeding on the nearby freeway. He hid between two cars on the closest of four lines of trains all sitting still in the depot.

Snake-man stepped out, boldly searching for the magician. A thunderous voice echoed from the car behind CJ.

"*You.*"

CJ jumped back toward the greasy connectors between the two metal cars. If Snake-man saw him, the Super wouldn't hesitate to attack, mistaking CJ for the magician.

"*Cannot.*" This one came from far up the line.

"*Defeat.*" A car in the middle.

"*Me.*" The magician threw his amplified voice from one car to the other. Snake-man turned toward the sound each time.

"*I. Will. Destroy. You!*"

Snake-man cracked his knuckles. If it came to blows, the magician wouldn't have a chance against the larger Super. The green scales acted like armor. The man was famous for grappling and squeezing his opponents into unconsciousness like a python.

"Not with a stupid puppet trick, you won't. Now step out here and fight like a man."

"While. You. Fight. Like. A. Reptile?" The cars on either side of CJ rumbled as part of the sentence.

"Whatever. If I have to search this whole place, I'll tear your arms off when I catch you cowering in one of these trains."

No response. CJ almost tripped on one of the rails as he moved to glance around the corner again. The snake poked his head into one open car, pulling back out a second later. He moved away from CJ toward the front of the train, checking each opening.

Another magnesium flare, brighter than the noon sun, exploded from a freight car the instant the snake entered it, momentarily casting a giant shadow of the Super against the ground and stacks of junk near the rails.

The blind Snake-man stepped back just as Jakak donkey-kicked him in the face with the heel of a shiny tuxedo shoe. Bad move. Before the magician recovered, Snake-man lashed out and grabbed his foot.

The smaller man pulled away, leaving only a shoe in the huge hands. Blinking rapidly, the snake pulverized the Italian leather and tossed aside the black shards. "Give it up, villain. All your tricks won't save you."

"What makes you think I'm the villain?" asked Jakak. His voice no longer jumped from car to car. Now it seemed to come from everywhere at once. "You're the one bullying people all over Denver. You're the corporate shill, taking money from beer companies to endorse the depressants people use to self-medicate and ignore the oppression they live under."

"Is that your power? You talk at people until they fall asleep?"

"Why Denver? Why not New York or some other Gothic city?"

"Denver needs me." The snake's head darted from one possible hiding place to another, searching for the source.

"To save them from the clutches of the scientist who was working on alternative clean energy fuels?"

"He blew up an apartment building."

"Only because he couldn't get legitimate funding from a short-sighted and narrow-minded government."

Snake-man scoffed. "Whatever. He was a mad scientist and a menace, just like you. I have to protect the city from all your kind."

"The long arm of the fascist law."

CJ usually stopped listening when Supers started bickering about their causes. It had nothing to do with him. He had to listen now for clues about where they were and what would happen next. With any luck, he'd be able to help the magician beat the snake and get hired full time. Timing was always tricky.

Snake-man jumped into the first car on the train.

The muscleman smashed his fists into the metal wall, rocking the train all the way back.

"Poor Snake-man. Always the underdog. Always trying to prove snakes are every bit as scary as bats and spiders."

"Shut-up! When I'm done with you, I'm going to toss your corpse off the new skyscraper downtown, Jak-ass!"

"Oooh! A pun. I would expect no less from a frustrated football player with a bad knee."

"Not any more. I have a purpose now. And I'm going to kick you from…"

Sounds echoed from the top of the train. CJ ran to the train waiting on the next set of tracks, turning to look on top of the first one. The magician walked atop the freight car. His one shoe and one wet sock making distinct sounds amplified by the big metal box. He'd been in the car next to CJ the whole time? How did CJ not hear him moving across a sheet-metal floor in hard-soled shoes or climbing the ladder?

With the dimming sun to his back, the magician raised his wand and blasted a fountain of purple fireworks at Snake-man. The action was too close. CJ looked for somewhere to run without being seen.

Ignoring the small sparks, the green-clad Super made one big jump to the top of the train, reaching out to grab the magician.

CJ stepped around the corner and punched Snake-man in the gut. The costumed man's beefy hand came loose from Jakak's shoe. The snake turned toward CJ.

3

Jakak winked at CJ and disappeared again. Snake-man tried to kick CJ as he held the corner of the train car to keep from tumbling to the ground. CJ dodged and ran behind the car, looking for a new place to duck out of sight. The magician, taking advantage of the diversion, stomped down with a plastic heel on his opponent's hand. The snake fell to the ground. A giant metal tube, like the ones CJ had been hiding behind before, crashed down on top.

"Aaaargh!" Snake-man screamed as if a demon possessed him. "My back. I can't…"

The magician appeared next to the green mess, twisted at odd angles and held down by thousands of pounds of steel. He pulled off his hat with a wicked grin. "Snakes were cursed in the Garden of Eden. That's why nobody's afraid of you."

The wounded man spit at the only part of his enemy he could, the last shoe.

Before the acid burned through, the magician stomped down on the scaly hood with it, knocking the Snake-man out. Then he kicked the shoe off.

Once the man confirmed his adversary wouldn't be getting up, he stumbled away. Despite the bravado, the magician limped now that he thought nobody could see him.

CJ stepped out. "You should get the pants and sock off that foot, too," he said. "Even small drops of Snake-man's acid will burn through."

The magician paused, standing tall again. "You saw the battle?"

"Most of it."

"And you're not afraid I'll destroy you next?"

"No. I'm not a threat to you. In fact, I was hoping for a job." CJ pulled out a Swiss army knife and flipped it open. He cut the man's left pant leg off at the knee, ripping down the back seam and tossing the smoldering silk away.

One diamond cufflink sparkled in the pink sun as Jakak lifted his foot and slipped off both his socks. He shifted his weight from one foot to the other, the sharp and oily rocks causing him some discomfort. He sized CJ up. "You wish to be my famulus?"

CJ blinked. "I don't know what that is."

"My assistant, my servant."

"Ah. Well, if it comes with a paycheck…"

"I already have a famulus." CJ looked down at his shoes and nodded. "But I am looking for a few more. I will always have use of good men who aren't afraid to buck the system. You clearly aren't afraid of snakes."

CJ glanced past the barefoot magician to the unconscious Snake-man. "Never liked the guy."

"Very well." Jakak clicked the end of his wand like a pen. A ballpoint stuck out the other end. He pulled a blue business card out of his jacket with a picture of a magician on the front, and wrote a list on the back as he said, "Start by finding my hat. This is the address of my tailor. Please have him clean or repair my hat and get a new pair of pants and shoes for this suit. Tell him Jakak the Magnificent sent you. He has my sizes on file. Get a suit for yourself, too. Wear it when you bring my things to the address on the bottom."

CJ smiled. "You bet, boss. I'll go straight there after dinner."

CJ CRUZ STOPPED TO ADMIRE HIMSELF IN THE REFLECTION OF A STOREFRONT window. It usually took time to adjust to a new outfit on the first day of the job, but CJ liked this one immediately. Below the words painted on the glass and to the side of the posters, he found a nice reflective surface. He pulled his tuxedo jacket tight over the metallic blue cummerbund, tipping his top hat forward before tapping his shiny shoes with the end of a black cane.

"I hope Jakak stays around a while," CJ said to the woman with him. "I could get used to these classy outfits."

"You look like a monkey," Ana said. She pushed him aside with her shoulder and straightened her own long-tailed jacket. They had similar hats and canes, but she wore a ruffled shirt with lace sticking out the sleeves. Instead of pants, she wore white tights crossed by black fishnet. Her pink tinted hair didn't match the outfit. "I hate these costumes."

CJ found a smaller open area on the shiny surface and tucked a few stray brown hairs back into the hat. He'd shaved this morning, but he had a five o'clock shadow already. He wished he'd landed this gig ten years ago when he didn't have as much of a beer gut. When he looked up at his partner, he laughed. "It's better than the last time we worked together dressed like clowns. Remember your costume had those big—"

"Anything is better." She cupped her hands around her eyes so she could see into the dimly lit shop. "What kind of a name is Jakak anyway? You think his mother looked down at her cute little baby and said, 'He looks like a Jakak?'"

"Supers always change their names." CJ kept pulling out and tucking in one lock of hair to see which look he preferred.

"Maybe we should stop primping and get back to work?"

CJ shook his head. "Not this place. The profit margin on a comic book store is razor thin. One shake down would put them out of business."

Ana put her hand on one hip and popped it to the side, giving him a stink-eye stare worthy of his ex. "What do you care, you're just a lackey."

CJ held up one finger, his brows knit. "I'm nobody's lackey."

"What do you want to be called then? Henchman? Thug? What's the difference?"

"I'm an independent sub-contractor."

"What does that even mean?" Ana tapped her cane on the ground and looked past him like she'd grown bored with the conversation already.

"It means I get hired temporarily by various employers, but I maintain my own business." CJ didn't care if she didn't want to hear it, he wasn't about to let her get away with talking down to him about his job.

"It doesn't matter if you call them, 'ladies of the night', they are still whores." She scrunched up her nose like he smelled bad and walked past him.

CJ spun on his slick shoes and followed. He didn't like working with Ana. Ten years younger than him, she just took these jobs for cheap thrills. She didn't have any pride or long-term plans. Too many people like her in his profession had given them all a bad name... or three bad names.

"How about this one, Your Highness? Can we shake them down?"

"A dry cleaner? Really?"

"See that limo a block back?" Ana stared into his eyes through her purple contacts. CJ glanced over her shoulder. "Don't stare! That's our boss watching us."

CJ turned away and looked at the petite old woman hemming a pair of pants inside the shop. "So?"

"I don't know about you, but when I'm being watched, I like to look good. Unlike you, *independent sub-contractor*, I'm not planning to be a two-bit hoodlum my whole life. I'm going to work my way up and get in on the real action, and the real money. So either take me to a store you're okay with robbing, or stand out here while I explain why grandma there needs some new insurance."

CJ scoffed. "You want to work your way up to what? Being the boss's right hand man, or woman, is a death sentence in this business. The next Super to come along..."

"Bored now." Ana pushed past him and grabbed the door handle.

CJ put his cane in front of her. "Okay. Take it easy. There's a jewelry store down the street. They're much more likely to have a lot of cash on hand. The boss wants to make a statement. Can't do that in a ma-and-pa shop."

"You're such a loser." Ana let go, her heels clicking as she walked down the street.

CJ spun his cane around his wrist and followed her, keeping his head up. A mother pushed her stroller far to the side of the sidewalk, diverting her eyes as he passed. He tipped his hat to her with a smile anyway.

Ana stopped, her eyes wide. "You know we work for a Supervillain, right? We're the bad guys."

CJ walked right past her, head held high. "The whole notion of heroes and villains is outdated. They are all just Supers. The things they fight over don't really apply to us normals."

"You're delusional."

"Don't be daft." He put his hands out to each side. "I know what I am, but I draw the line at hurting innocent people for no reason. If Supers want to go at each other and pay for a little side help, I'm all for it. But I don't have any reason to ruin the lives of regular folks looking to get by, same as me."

"They are not like you." Ana rolled her eyes. "You think they'd do the same for you?"

CJ stopped in front of the jewelry store. It was part of a national chain. They'd have piles of insurance to cover the losses. He felt a lot better taking money away from huge corporations. "No, probably not. Doesn't matter. I'm in it for the long game, not some misguided attempt at fame."

"Shut up. Just don't get in my way here, or I promise I'll use this cane gun on you." She lifted the black crook and held it like a shotgun.

Kicking the door in, she yelled, "Hands up!"

"No, no, no!" CJ followed her in. The middle-aged man and mid-twenties woman on the other side of the glass counter had their arms high. The young woman kept glancing to the side of the display giving away the location of the alarm button.

The man in the cheap suit said, "Just take what you want. We won't resist." His thin body and pale skin were evidence of his sincerity.

"Empty the register!" Ana said it like they were auditioning her for a guest part in a cop show.

"Just relax." CJ gently pushed down on Ana's cane. "We don't want to hurt anybody. We are here on behalf of Jakak the Magnificent. He's going to change the world."

"You don't really have to say all that stuff." Ana pointed to the computer

and the man typed in the code to pop open the money tray.

The woman stepped away, toward the end of the counter. Ana picked up the cane and pointed it at her head. "Push that alarm, and you'll be a smear on the wall."

The man stepped away from the tray and CJ took off his hat. Did he have hat hair? Probably. He took the bills out of the tray, counting over a thousand bucks, and stuffed them into his hat. *Thou shalt not steal.* One second later, the money disappeared. CJ bit his lower lip. Why couldn't Supers ever make any money legitimately?

CJ turned the hat over and smiled, tipping it so the man could see. "It's empty. Isn't that cool? Jakak is the real deal. He's not just some phony illusionist. He really does magic."

The man rolled his eyes. "Yeah. That's great."

Ana lifted her cane and brought it down hard.

CJ thrust his out, stopping her before she broke through the glass display. "No need to make a mess."

"This is my share," Ana said. "You two, wallet and purse."

"No." CJ put out one hand. "We're done here." Ana stared poison daggers at him, but he wouldn't flex. He wasn't in this business to hurt the little people. "You're under me, so we do it my way. Jakak is getting his name out as a reformer, not a mafia boss."

Ana shook her head, and kicked the crash bar on the door as she left. CJ tipped his hat to the two behind the counter. "I did you a favor there." They both nodded, unsure if they should still be afraid. "Please do me one and don't hit that button for a minute or so. Okay?"

He couldn't see Ana on the street. She must have gone into one of the nearby stores for a solo shake down. The black limo pulled up. As the tinted window came down, Jakak said, "Nice work, CJ." The tall car had enough headroom for him to wear the card-decorated hat inside. "I appreciate your vision. Here's a bonus. Why don't you take the afternoon off and meet me tomorrow? I have some big plans."

CJ translated taking the afternoon off to mean get out of here before the cops show up. "Thanks!" He pocketed the bills without looking down. "Should I tell Ana?"

"I'll take care of it." The window slid up as the limo rolled forward. People all along the street watched them now. They'd made an impression for sure. CJ decided against the leisurely stroll he wanted and turned down the next alley. When distant sirens faded in, he ran.

"I invited your mom to join us, Juliet," CJ said to his daughter across the scant remains of a steak dinner. "She just doesn't like being around me."

"I know. Thanks for trying." She looked across the top of her glasses as she picked up her phone and quickly texted her friend. "So you got a new job?"

CJ saw so much of his ex in her. Blonde hair and a sharp nose with slightly darker skin like his, and her twelve-year-old brain made both her parents look dumb. "Not really. I always have the same job, but I depend on contractors and sometimes there's not work."

Juliet rolled her blue eyes and shook her head. "I'm not dumb, Daddy. I know you work for Supers."

CJ had a quick rebuke ready, but she knew him too well to say "villain" as part of his job. "Exactly. I'm no different from a plumbing sub-contractor. They get hired by builders to install the pipes in a new building. If nobody calls, they don't have any pipes to put in for a while."

"It's a little different." She smiled when her eyes caught something on her phone. She tapped a few times and looked right back at him. "I'm glad you have a builder again."

"So, how's Lexi fixed for cash these days?"

"What do you mean?" Juliet waved out the window at some girls from her school.

"Do you guys have enough money?"

"Does anybody ever have enough?"

"Good point." She obviously didn't know or wouldn't tell him. "At least she let me see you tonight."

She opened her eyes wide and asked, "Are we still on for Saturday?"

"The museum. Of course. Well, hopefully. I don't know the new work schedule yet. But we'll go soon. If I can't make it then, I'll call when I know."

Juliet jumped up, pulling on her jacket. "Mom said I have to get back in time to finish my homework."

CJ nodded, smiling despite feeling sad at taking her home after such a short visit. At least the ex had let him take her at all tonight. She usually didn't like last minute plans, even for small celebrations like getting a new job.

They walked a block back to Juliet's apartment. The sun dropped, causing CJ to zip up his jacket. "Are you warm enough?"

"I'm fine." She rolled her eyes. "So did you think about it yet?"

"Think about what?"

She gave an audible huff, just like Lexi. "I asked if I could come to your work one day and see what you do."

"Oh, yeah. Well, maybe. With a new boss, I have to get a feel for what's up before I know for sure."

"It's for a school assignment, so it has to be pretty soon. Otherwise,

I'll have to go watch Mom at the newspaper. I've done it tons of times. It's sooooo boring." Juliet's whole body rose and fell to emphasize the extremity of boredom.

"Did you tell her you wanted to see me at work?"

"Are you kidding?" One eyebrow lifted as she looked at him like he just suggested she cut off her own hand. "I'm not stupid."

"No, you definitely aren't." CJ rubbed his bristled chin. "I'll tell you what, I'll let you know. Maybe I can squeeze something in on Saturday and we postpone the museum?"

"Okay, but we have to go to the museum sometime this month. The Superhero display is only there for a while."

CJ forced a smile. He wanted to see the display just for research purposes. They arrived at the door of the stucco covered three-story apartment building. "I'll wait here until you get inside. Could you give this to your mom? I know I've been behind lately, but this should catch me up. Sorry I couldn't get it in time for new school clothes."

Juliet took the bills and stuffed them into her jacket pocket. The corner of a hundred-dollar bill still stuck out the side. CJ resisted the temptation to tell her to tuck it in all the way. She said, "Thanks. And thanks for dinner."

He hugged her a long time. "Thanks for celebrating with me." He gave her a kiss on the forehead before she went up a half-flight of stairs. She waved back at him, disappearing through the door.

CJ let the smile drop.

The apartment manager's door on the first floor opened, and out came a sixty-year-old woman with the face of a dinosaur. She'd begun to hunch over, but she still struck terror into CJ. Why hadn't he bolted after the hug?

"Cold out here, CJ," the woman said, as if even those words were a command.

"Yes, Mrs. Herriman. I should get going so I don't get sick."

She reached out a shriveled little hand, like a tyrannosaurus claw, to stop him. "Not so fast. You're behind on your share of the rent. I'd hate to have to throw that sweet little girl of yours out on the street."

"Lexi pays the rent," CJ said. "I don't live here anymore."

"I see. Then I'll just tell her the price went up last year. Okay, goodbye." She turned, without lowering her claw.

"Wait." CJ dropped his eyes. He pulled out the rest of his cash and held it out. Mrs. Herriman grabbed the wad faster than a cat and licked her thumb to count through it.

Thou shalt not lie. A year ago, the hag told him she raised the rent. He already knew Lexi couldn't afford to live here on a proofreader's salary and his pitiful child support. She sacrificed food, clothes, everything to stay in this neighborhood so Juliet could have better schools. Even divorced, his ex had a way of making him feel like a waste of human life. So he covered the raise in rent to spare her pride and keep his daughter with her friends."Bit short," Mrs. Herriman said.

"It's all I got."

4

"A wizard-duel?" CJ held onto his top hat so he could shake his head without it falling off. They were standing near some aspen trees along the west side of Cornerstone Park. A wide expanse of green grass where seven football fields clustered together held only a few people playing Frisbee and a woman tossing a tennis ball for her dog to fetch.

Ana smirked. "That's what the boss said. We're not to interfere unless she brings in help. Then we are only supposed to fight the lackeys."

"She?" CJ had been glad Ana got the job as head assistant instead of him being in the crosshairs, but he wished she'd be a little more forthcoming with details about their current assignment.

"I thought you knew all the Super folks and their powers." She moved over to the grass so her high heels wouldn't keep sticking into the ground. It didn't help.

CJ shielded his eyes from the sun to see if he could detect anybody waiting in the fringes on the far side. "I try to keep up on the business, but that doesn't mean I know who's in town at the moment. You were the one in the super-secret boss meeting, so spill it."

"Spelladonna. Even I've heard of that one."

It made sense. She was a fringe Super who, as the name suggested, worked with poison. Some said it was magical, others just chemistry. It didn't seem like a good power for dueling. He wished he had a phone so he could look her up while they waited. "She usually has a bunch of followers with her. We're supposed to hold them off with just two people?"

"That's why we got upgraded sticks." She lifted her black cane and pointed to a button on the bottom. "This batch is actually guns."

CJ examined the button and open end of a barrel. "Thanks for telling me. I could have fired it on accident."

"They only have six shots, so don't waste any." She twirled it like a drum major's baton. "About time we got a job with some serious equipment."

A group of women in slinky purple dresses came out onto the far corner of the field. "Heads up." CJ sighed. "Six women and Spelladonna. Great. With all the local muscle-for-hire in prison thanks to Doctor Pain, she must have brought them with her when she came to town."

"Don't tell me you're too much of a gentleman to fight a girl."

"The odds concern me more." *Thou shalt not lie.* CJ felt his stomach tighten. It wasn't the gender or the odds that bothered him.

Ana started marching forward in shoes as unpractical as their opponents'. His tuxedo shoes would give him a slight advantage, but he really wished he'd worn something athletic.

"Where's Jakak?" asked Spelladonna when they were within shouting distance.

"He'll show up when it's just you two, one on one." Ana stood with her feet shoulder width apart, leaning on the black cane.

"And you monkeys?" Spelladonna asked.

"We're just here to make sure your friends have company during the negotiations."

CJ looked at his partner. Ana didn't usually employ tact. Maybe being chief assistant suited her. Of course, the title would have more meaning if there was more than a pair of them.

Spelladonna scanned the area. She had big, jeweled rings on every finger. A necklace dripping with sparkles matched broad, hanging earrings. A few sprigs of baby's breath poked out of her hair. Her followers wore fewer accessories. "You really think just the two of you can take six acolytes on your own?"

CJ shrugged. "I'm not great at math. How many acolytes equals one famulus again?"

Ana scowled at him, turning her attention back to their foes. "As soon as

you're ready, feel free to step away from your puppies."

"Burn!" CJ laughed.

Spelladonna looked at him like he had the plague. CJ laughed hard enough to snort. Honestly, he hoped she'd attack him directly. Then he could just shoot her and save everybody the trouble.

Jakak's voice boomed from nowhere. *"Step away from the witch!"*

CJ and Ana moved to the south. Spelladonna nodded to her support group. They also moved to the south. One of them squinted her eyes at CJ, pointing with a crooked finger and muttering under her breath.

"Bibbity-bobbity-boo!" CJ held up the cane like a long wand.

"Stop being an idiot," Ana said, pulling on his arm. "What happened to being so glad you finally got to wear a tux and work for a classy boss?"

"I don't like this," he said. *Thou shalt not kill.* "I don't want to gun down a pack of women. I hired on to fight Supers, not slaughter normals."

"Then pull out your little prayer beads and hope they don't start anything, because if you don't have my back, I'll shoot you myself."

"Great pep-talk from the boss's pet. I'll do my job, but I'm not killing anybody." CJ turned with the rest to look at Spelladonna.

Red fireworks exploded in a circle around the sorceress. Daylight diminished the impact of the visual effect. When the smoke cleared, five images of Jakak stood in a circle around the woman in purple.

"You came all this way for nothing," five Jakaks said in unison. "There's no vacancy for a two-bit illusionist in Denver."

"Then you better go back to Vegas." She spread her fingers, several colored gems gleaming in the sun. Vines leaped from the ground, circling the feet of all the magicians around her. Four of them disappeared.

Jakak tipped his cane and burned through the vine with red fire, which also singed his pants. CJ knew he'd be heading to the tailor again tomorrow. Thorns kept the severed length of plant attached to one black pant leg.

The vine continued to grow from the ground, searching blindly, like a green tentacle, for a victim. Jakak faded out and reappeared ten feet away. He pulled the small wand out of his jacket and raised it high.

A bolt of lightning fell from the clear sky. Spelladonna jumped to the side, crossing her arms over her chest. The bolt reflected and leaped for Jakak.

Blue tinted electricity shot through Jakak's holographic image. The bolt continued until it reached the ground and singed the grass between Ana and the closest acolyte.

More vines burst from the ground. These had bright red flowers with long, fingerlike petals. They curled back and began shooting streams of thick liquid.

Jakak jumped a few times, avoiding the spray. "How many plants have to die for you today?" He swiped his cane, sending jets of agro out over the attacking flora. The accelerant ignited, roasting the vines and sending up plumes of black smoke wherever a flower ignited.

"That depends how long you intend to keep this up." She wiggled her fingers and the grass began to grow around Jakak's shoes.

CJ, intrigued by the battle, began thinking it might just be settled by the two Supers. He really hoped Jakak would win. From the look of things, Ana had a job either way, but he'd be out of work again if Jakak lost.

"I don't think it will take long," the magician said. He tapped the ground and a circle around him glowed red and turned black, the grass flash burning to ash. "You're no match for me."

As soon as Spelladonna answered, CJ knew his hopes had been in vain. "Sisters, attack!"

5

Six banshees in purple dresses and high heels all started wailing at the same time.

CJ didn't wait for them to finish. Guilt or no guilt, he wasn't about to let them get to the end of whatever curse they started. He jumped forward, both arms out, and plowed into the whole mob like a human bowling ball.

Ana had her cane up, ready to start shooting, but once CJ got in the way, she apparently decided not to risk taking out her only ally, and joined the melee.

Unarmed, Spelladonna's acolytes kicked and elbowed in unison. Sooner or later, one of them would make him into a soprano. Being a choirboy ranked among his best-kept childhood secrets, and he had no intention of going back. He pushed up, tucked his feet under, and jumped forward, rolling out of the mess of flailing females.

His fearless leader jumped in when he left, stomping on women and kicking any she missed. She hit a few with the cane, but got better results with her heavy shoes.

A couple of women rolled out of the floundering pile. One lunged at CJ with sharp fingernails. She managed to scratch his hand before he twirled the cane around and beat her wrists away. He could feel the abrasions itching immediately. A very bad sign.

Ana stepped on one woman's stomach and jumped on the second who had managed to right herself, rushing off to help her mistress. When Ana

brought her down head first, the woman didn't get up again.

CJ tried to ignore the stinging cuts as he wielded the cane like a sword and began smacking any fingers he saw reaching up. When he had a chance, he also conked a few upside the head.

One woman, crouching, managed to finish a string of nonsense words, her voice rising to a shrill crescendo. Ropes burst from the ground, tying Ana's wrists and waist, pulling her face down into the grass.

Before she could stand up or start another spell, CJ punched her in the back of the head. She went out cold.

He surveyed their six opponents: three unconscious and three moaning on the ground. Seeing no immediate threat, he pulled out his knife and began to cut Ana free. Two of the women rose up on their hands, he didn't have time to finish, so he turned his cane on the thickest part of the fibers and shot through it into the ground.

The women began making hand gestures and mumbling. CJ grabbed Ana's cane and swung both at the same time. The chanters both leaned back, but the long canes still managed to knock their heads together.

One fell. The other, shaky, rushed CJ.

With two long sticks in his hands, CJ couldn't pull his arms back in time to defend himself. The woman impacted him with both elbows on his shoulders and her knee in his gut. He went down with her sprinting over the top.

He gasped for air, filling a collapsed lung, glad she hadn't been shorter. He rolled to see the woman sprinting toward the Supers, knowing he'd never be able to stop her before she reached them.

The woman dropped. Next to him, Ana had one of the canes held up like a rifle. She pulled another strand of vine from one of her wrists as she turned on the rest of their enemies.

Being distracted with his own fight, CJ had almost forgotten the Supers battling it out nearby. The grass had huge patches of black where fire scorched it. Strange stumps and branches stuck out at odd angles. Jakak had Spelladonna down, with his cane across her neck. If any of her acolytes had gotten there, she could have changed the outcome.

CJ grabbed the last cane and pointed it at the only two women sitting up in the group before him. "Yes, these are guns. Don't make a single sound, or I will shoot you." *Thou shalt not lie.* He shook his head. *Not now!*

Backing away, he could hear Jakak talking to the subdued Super. "You will never come back to Denver, or next time, I will not be so merciful."

CJ smiled. After all this time, he was finally working for one of the good guys. His hand burned, though. He looked at the three short red lines in his hand. They were puffing up and the red spread toward his wrist.

When one of the women they had covered pointed to the fallen sister and made big eyes, Ana nodded once. The woman rushed over and began taking care of the gunshot wound.

Ana looked at CJ. "That was a pretty good move. Still, it would have been easier just to shoot them all in the legs."

"Hate to spoil such nice legs. Besides, it's their mouths you gotta watch out for. And the claws." He sucked in a deep breath and blew on the back of his hand to try and cool it.

"That's ugly," she said. She pulled a flask out of her jacket and held it out.

CJ dropped his cane and poured the clear alcohol over the red stripes.

New pain shot up his arm and made him see stars. When he could talk again he asked, "What is that, 180 proof?"

"It's a small flask."

The women began to regroup. CJ walked backward, keeping an eye on them as he left with Jakak and Ana.

"Well done, boss," she said as they neared the trees.

"Barbaric, but necessary. I couldn't have succeeded without your help." He took his hat off and shook his head.

"What's wrong?" CJ asked.

"We need to get the message out," Jakak said. "We need to reach more people."

CJ shrugged. "So you want to hijack a news station?" He liked that this guy was focused, even after a brawl.

"No, something to attract more attention." The magician looked around the miniature golf course to their right.

"Like an amusement park?" CJ indicated the waterslides across the street.

"Too gauche. Maybe a bank."

"A bank job?" CJ snorted. Some things never changed. One way or another, it always came down to the same thing.

6

Jakak held up his wand, with his new metallic cape rippling behind him. He stood in the middle of the bank, where all the cameras could see him at once.

"I will bring down the machine of oppression! Join me in standing up against those who would exploit the poor. We have the power if we just take it back!"

Thou shalt not steal. CJ sighed. Did it count as stealing if they were just doing a fund-raiser for a good cause? He held out his hat as the teller handed over cash from the till. It disappeared into the blackness. He smiled, trying to calm her.

Ana jabbed the man across the counter with her cane. "Now the vault."

Shaking, the man said, "We can't access the money in the vault."

"I can see it right there," she pointed with her free hand. "It's wide open."

"But the money is in a locked drop box inside." He pointed toward the round opening. "It can only open when the security guys come to empty it."

"That's a lie." Ana sneered.

"It's not, actually." CJ shrugged. "They only keep about ten thousand out. The rest gets regularly locked up where nobody can get to it."

Ana glared with murderous rage. She spun on the teller and said, "Just get what you have out!"

Jakak shot red sparks from his wand as he waved his other white glove dramatically. "Don't feed the beast. Starve it out by refusing to join in the rampant consumerism they use to enslave you."

When the money ran out, CJ and Ana stepped away from the counter. Sirens howled outside. CJ raised his eyebrows. "Time to go, boss?"

"Never leave the stage early," Jakak said with a flourish. "Everybody in this room is now my hostage. Please sit down in front of the counter."

Ana slapped one white glove against her face. "Our jail time just tripled."

A security guard rushed in, hand on his belt. Though she probably went for a Tazer, CJ couldn't take the risk. He swung his walking stick in a wide arc.

The woman fell to the ground in a heap after the white tip of the black rod bounced off the side of her skull

Jakak pulled a bouquet of red roses out of his sleeve and handed one to each of the tellers and unfortunate customers as they sat on the floor in a line. CJ knew how to do some rudimentary magic. Normally those flowers would be hidden up the magician's sleeve, but not Jakak's. He could really pull things out of thin air. CJ expected when the time came, the magician would just make all three of them disappear, right before the police officers' eyes. At least he hoped so.

"Come out with your hands up!" called a stern voice through a bullhorn. Several cop cars slid to a stop parallel to the sidewalk. The officers jumped out and set up behind them, holding guns across the hood and trunk. The tinted glass windows of the bank let them see straight through to the hostage situation.

Jakak smiled at his assistants. Then he walked out the front door with his hands up. For anybody else, it would be a gesture of surrender, but CJ knew better.

Two officers ran forward with guns up. One dangled handcuffs from her other hand. Before they came close, Jakak exploded.

Green fireworks blasted in every direction, blinding everybody who looked and showering copper sparks all over the building, cars, and officers.

"Everybody down!" CJ yelled as he dived behind the now penniless counter.

The two cops in front fell back as the other three opened fire, shooting round after round at Jakak's chest.

The bullets passed through the mirage, shattering the bank's two glass doors and riddling the wall and counter behind. All the hostages screamed. Ana, who hadn't listened to CJ's advice, jumped behind a loan consultation desk, with her fishnet legs flailing up behind her.

In accordance with their training, the cops kept shooting at the image of a man who would not fall down. When their magazines emptied, the thunderous reports stopped, leaving only the tinkle of falling glass shards.

Jakak laughed. In a blur, he stepped to the side, dropping his hands and posing as he leaned on his cane. He wore a huge, innocent smile. "Missed me."

The police reached for spare clips as a new round of pyrotechnics blasted forward. This time, the golden rockets were more than a show. Each one hit a policeman's head or chest with perfect accuracy, knocking all of them away from the cars.

"Only three cars? You underestimate my power." A purple eldritch light began to glow on the hood and roof of each squad car, bright enough to be seen in the daylight. The dancing fires blackened and bubbled the paint, then dripped through to the inside.

"Run!" called one cop through the bullhorn. Those still conscious crawled away from the violet flames. A few dragged their unconscious companions away.

The closest car exploded. Jakak pointed with his white tipped stick as it went off. Less dramatic than the giant fireballs in movies, this blast only lifted the hood and sent fire rising out the sides. The interior filled with black smoke, which leaked out and rose diagonally into the wind.

Jakak turned his cane to point at the next car as it exploded.

Then the third, right on time like an orchestra conductor. "I bear no hard feelings to you pawns of the dictators. Your loyalty is merely misguided. One day I will make you marshals over a peaceful state, where your efforts are appreciated instead of mocked openly in the news by protestors who don't understand that you are just the messenger of oppression, not the source."

A news van screeched to a stop half a block away. A camera operator and reporter jumped out the back and worked their way cautiously forward, already rolling film.

Jakak smiled. "Finally!"

One of the police officers lifted his gun and fired between the trails of smoke.

This time the bullets didn't pass through, they diverted to each side, cutting new holes into the bank's glass walls and bringing up a new round of screams from the people cowering inside.

Jakak's smile dropped as he pulled out a second, smaller wand and pointed it at the man. The officer's uniform instantly burst into flames. He screamed as three of his group swatted at the fire, which rapidly spread to their sleeves. He rolled across the ground ineffectually.

"I am the voice of the underdog, but I will not tolerate disrespect." Jakak turned back toward the camera, lifting his wand. His voice projected louder than the bullhorn. "I am Jakak the Magnificent. I have come to liberate the poor and downtrodden."

The reporter moved forward and stepped into the shot. She began talking to the camera, leaving plenty of room for the viewers to see the scene behind her.

Jakak pointed at CJ and Ana. Through the shattered door he said, "Time to join me."

The forgotten hostages all stood up among the shards of glass and crouch-walked through the swinging door to the improved safety behind the counter. CJ straightened his bowtie and put on his hat. Ana rolled her eyes and just walked out into the street.

The car fires dwindled. Several officers had reloaded guns pointing at them, but nobody said anything. Jakak moved around the smoldering car husks. CJ and Ana followed.

"These two have joined my cause already, helping to lash out against the uber-rich who constantly siphon money away from the working classes to pay for their decadence and debauchery. As proof of my good intentions, I will never consent to rule you. I will only work to release you from your bonds so others can take the reins of prosperity!"

The reporter, growing bold, walked toward Jakak for an interview.

Two fiery streaks raced into the sky. CJ unceremoniously tugged on Jakak's jacket sleeve. Jakak turned on him, furious, until he saw what CJ indicated. The fiery lines changed course, catching more attention from anybody looking up.

Jakak strolled toward the camera, speaking faster now, "Here come two of the oppressors' guard dogs now. They claim to be heroes, but they only defend the corrupt leaders. Do not respect those who…"

The camera pointed toward the approaching streaks of fire. Jakak's voice trailed off when he realized he'd lost his coverage.

As they neared, colors resolved and CJ could clearly see the leader wore red and the one behind brown. The halos of fire parting around them widened as they slowed before landing. The two came down right in the street, halfway between Jakak and the cinematographer.

They crashed into the asphalt, sending up a cloud of dust and leaving two craters in the middle of a spider-web of cracks radiating across the road.

"Who's that?" Ana asked quietly.

CJ rolled his eyes. "You really should keep up with these things if you're going to survive in this business."

She punched him in his well-dressed arm.

"Alright. It's Shooting Star and his sidekick, Meteoric-man."

The Super-duo stepped over the ridge of rubble they'd made and posed, standing tall with fists on their hips and flexed abs. Red and brown capes flowed behind them in the wind, accenting the matching white logos on their chests. Their eyes showed through red-and brown ninja masks.

Shooting Star said, "It's curtain time for you, Jakak."

Ana moaned. CJ laughed.

Jakak held up his wand and cane, blasting lines of blue fire toward both the newcomers. Meteoric-man leaped to the side and rolled. Shooting Star stayed in place, letting the chemical heat splash over him until it burned out.

"Fighting fire with fire is my trick, Trickster." He raised his bare hands and wide cones of bright yellow fire burst out of them.

CJ grabbed Ana's collar and leaped away. Jakak stood still, letting Shooting Star's flames toast and then melt his black silhouette. When the burning stopped, only a charred pile of dust and bones suggested anyone had even been there.

When the heat dissipated, SS flew forward and bent over to examine the remains. Jakak materialized behind him and kicked the Super in the cape covered butt.

Shooting Star landed face first in the asphalt. Jakak stepped away from the top berm of the crater. "These so-called protectors are financed by big-oil to keep people like me from upsetting the system they feed off like vampires."

Seeing the camera lens spin for a close-up, Jakak lifted his cane and posed. "Do not let the corporate shills speak or act for you!"

CJ patted a small wad of the bank's cash he'd pocketed instead of dropping into the bottomless hat. Sometimes bosses needed help with the accounting. They became easily distracted from small matters like paychecks.

Meteoric-man leaped from the side, wrapping his arms around Jakak's waist to tackle him. CJ jumped out of the way again. The brown suited man flew straight through the illusion, landing hard where CJ had been just before.

"Take him out, Famuli!"

Ana looked at CJ. He nodded. "That's us."

She pointed her cane at Meteoric-man and pulled the trigger as he stood up.

The large man grabbed his abs and doubled over.

"Gut-shot. That's cruel. Legs or shoulders are kinder." CJ had his own cane up.

"Shut-up." Ana spun her cane with two hands in a wide arc over her head. At the last second, Shooting Star kicked her feet out from under her and she toppled.

CJ knew the critical moment in a Super-fight. His mind instantly cranked through everything he knew about the three involved here. If Jakak won this battle, CJ needed to appear loyal to keep his job. If the others won, CJ would probably spend the rest of his life in jail. Snake-man was an amateur compared to these two. They were famous all over America. When Shooting Star jumped fifty feet in the air, CJ knew what to do.

Shooting Star rocketed down toward Jakak and pounded into the magician's head. Of course, he passed right through the illusion, but the new crater, somewhat smaller than the first, still knocked the nearby wizard down. No longer invisible, Jakak landed on his butt three feet away.

CJ stepped up to Meteoric-man, fists raised in boxing position. He'd left his cane-gun on the ground and his knife in his pocket on purpose. Grateful his boss sent them after the sidekick, he feinted with the left and then punched straight into the cloth-covered eye.

Meteoric-man stumbled once, forgetting his bullet wound. He flexed his huge muscles and popped CJ right in the jaw.

CJ didn't block. Twisting his neck the instant before the hit took most of the power out of the punch. CJ fell anyway, landing hard on the concrete sidewalk, and tearing several holes in his tuxedo.

Ana jumped up to carry on the fight, landing a roundhouse kick with her high-heels right in the brown spandex torso.

CJ stayed down, feigning unconsciousness as he watched the rest of the battle.

Even as Meteoric-man's ribs cracked, the Super grabbed Ana's leg and leaped into the air. When they were three stories up, he dropped her. She fell as he tucked into a cannonball and crashed down on Jakak.

The sorcerer managed to roll out of the direct blast, but again the crater knocked him down. His bowtie hung to one side and his trademark hat flew off.

A dozen red rockets shot ten feet out from the magician and then exploded into thick clouds of red gas. Meteoric-man coughed violently as they both disappeared behind the shroud. Ana fell hard on the road and didn't move again before the breeze covered her in the bloody fog.

More sirens whined in the distance.

Shooting Star leaped into the air, fire blasting from both hands.

Shooting Star whistled as he started his re-entry. This final attack would be the end of Jakak. As soon as the first tendrils of the red cloud blew past him, CJ jumped up, leaving his hat, cane, and jacket behind as he ran.

CJ was going to miss those nice suits.

7

Forgive me, Father, for I have sinned. It's been one week since my last confession." CJ had his Broncos hat and black hoodie on again. He zipped it up because Father Weaver kept the Church of Saint Augustine cold. CJ liked it that way. It seemed to go with all the candles and stained glass windows. He couldn't see them from inside the closet-sized confessional, though.

Father Weaver couldn't keep the exasperation out of his voice. "What have you done now, CJ?"

The confessor tipped his head. "Shouldn't you call me, 'my child,' or something?"

The priest didn't answer, shaking his head.

"Well, I stole some money from a bank. Oh, and a jewelry store. But I didn't keep the money so it doesn't really count. Actually, that's a lie. I kept a little bit of the money, but only my fair pay plus a reasonable severance stipend, and that should have come out of Jakak's account anyway."

A long pause. A deep breath. "Is that all?"

"I lied to my wife. Ex-wife, and not directly. I still haven't told her about the rent hike. And I lied to my daughter. I told her I'd ask my boss if she could come to work with me on Saturday. But I didn't. Since that job ended suddenly, I'm going to get stuck going to the museum instead. So, technically it's not a lie, but it was when I told it."

"Is that all?"

"Just the usual lust, but we didn't fornicate or commit adultery. Delia's a good Catholic-girl. So that has to count for something, right?"

"Sure," the priest said. His voice had less timbre in it these days. "Anything else?"

"Maybe coveting. I really liked wearing a tuxedo, you know? Not likely to get another job with costumes that fancy. Well, except your job. But I don't think I could take four more years of school."

Father Weaver snorted. "Is that all?"

"I choked a guy. Also, I punched another guy. And hit several women. Is that a sin?"

"Depends who and why."

"A bar bouncer, some of Spelladonna's followers, and Meteoric-man. But MM hit me right back, sooo…"

"CJ, what do you expect me to say here?"

CJ looked at the intricately carved wooden screen between them. "Me? The usual, I suppose. Assign me some prayers and stuff so I don't feel guilty anymore."

"What's the point?"

"The point is to keep my soul clean so when I die I can go to heaven." CJ liked easy questions. He didn't like feeling guilty all the time, but his mother told him nobody got to heaven any other way.

"Until the next time you hire on as a thug?"

"Personal assistant. It's my job. It's what I do."

"Repentance is meant to help you improve. It's meant to help you change, to be a better person."

"Right, so my sins are gone."

"Wrong. So you stop sinning. I told you before, Pope Francis just ex-communicated the Mafia."

"Yes, you did. But I don't work for the Mafia. I work for Supers."

"Villains! You work for Supervillains."

CJ hated that word, but he couldn't be angry at a priest. It seemed wrong. Instead, he decided to explain. "The labels of hero and villain are artificial. Supers are their own thing. They don't follow the same rules as you and me. Most people don't realize Supers all think they are heroes and the other guys are their villains. The media likes to label them one way or the other, but it's all much more complicated than black and white.

"Take the guy I just worked for, Jakak the Magnificent. They called him a villain and Shooting Star a hero. But Shooting Star is financed by big-oil, the same ones who pollute the world and waste billions of dollars on mansions and yachts while poor people starve. Maybe his methods weren't legal, but Jakak really believed he was going to make things better for the little guys. He really had the same ideas as Jesus."

Father Weaver gasped. "Did you just compare a Supervillain magician to Jesus?"

CJ stopped to think about it. In many ways, Jesus and the saints were a lot like Supers. Maybe they were something more than Supers. He'd never thought of it before. He knew the priest would not be okay with the idea, though. "I didn't mean it like that."

"Let's talk out there," the priest said.

CJ went out the door and into the brightly colored chapel. A large crucifix up front behind the podium drew his attention immediately. The thorns and blood on the stained wood statue still provoked a visceral response after all these years. CJ scanned the candles in front of it to make sure the one he'd lit just before the confession still burned.

Father Weaver stood taller and thinner than CJ, his white collar the only thing breaking up the black garb. He said, "Whatever you yourself think, CJ, everybody else believes what you do is just like the Mafia. Most of the people who run around with Supervillains, or whatever you call them, are bad people. And they always make you do bad things."

"Like Ana." CJ nodded. He wasn't surprised. Most people feared Supers and didn't even try to understand them. "But it's the only thing I'm good at."

"I'm sure there are other jobs out there. You're better than this, CJ."

"Bagging groceries or stocking shelves maybe. I can't make enough to pay rent on that. I don't have any other skills, but I don't think God would want me to stop supporting Juliet."

"No. But he does want you to be a good person." The priest put one hand on CJ's shoulder. "And you can't be a good person while you're doing bad things."

CJ nodded. He tried to be as good as he could under the circumstances, saving the jewelry store clerks from giving Ana their wallet and purse, for example, but maybe that didn't add up to taking the money in the first place. Usually confession made him feel better for a while. This time, it was making things worse.

"I know you're a good person on the inside," Father Weaver said. "I know you mean well, and you're struggling with these issues ever since…"

CJ turned to make eye contact. Would the priest dare to say it?

"…ever since your father." There it was.

"It's not that," CJ said. "I got past that. It's just…"

"Just what?"

"I don't know. It's all so amazing what they can do. And even though I'm not one of them, I feel like I belong with them. They have all this power. Anything else seems pointless by comparison."

Father Weaver took CJ's shoulders and held them as he looked into the shorter man's eyes. "It doesn't matter how much power you have. The important part is how you use what you've been given."

CJ thought about those words. Was he just wasting his time? He couldn't accept such an idea. "Maybe I can't have their powers, but I can be a part of it as long as I stay out of the spotlight and…"

The priest dropped his hands, keeping eye contact. "Why can't you work with a hero then? Do something people can be proud of."

CJ shook his head and looked toward the candles. "Heroes have side-kicks. They don't hire help. And besides, they aren't really heroes."

"Okay. Well, just think about what I said. I'm letting you stay in the church for now, because I know you aren't technically in the Mafia and you are trying to do good. But be warned, CJ. The Pope might come out any time and excommunicate all the Supervillain gangs. If he does, I can't help you."

CJ swallowed hard. His mother taught him, above all else make sure you go to heaven. Whatever else happens in this life, if you go to hell, it's forever. CJ gulped again. "Any word from your higher ups on the divorce?"

Father Weaver sighed. "Well, she wasn't Catholic. Since it was her decision to end it, we have a little bit of wiggle room. I think they will probably leave it up to me, but these things take time. It would look better if you had a normal job."

An old woman came into the church, letting in the afternoon light for a few minutes, breaking the spell of the dimly lit holy room. The priest leaned in to CJ and whispered, "Two-hundred Hail Marys and eight-hundred Our Fathers."

"A thousand?" CJ's mouth hung open. That would take hours.

"Can't I show my best lady a good time once in a while?" CJ asked.

Delia stood before him with her hands on her hips. Her hair was tinted red and she wore a blouse and sweater, too nice for the Lucky Break Bail Bonds place he picked her up at after work. The green neon dollar signs flashed in the store window behind her, giving a strange glow to the night sky. She looked at him with dark brown eyes. Those eyes made him happy or sad with a glance. "Keeping a job for more than a week would be the best time you could show me."

"It was a pretty great gig." He reached out his hand and she took it. They walked away from her work, passing storefronts as cars passed them. She knew exactly what he did for a living, and she seemed okay with it. He wasn't going to make the same mistake of hiding it as he had with his ex. "I'm sure something will come up soon. SS and MM are too big of names to stay in Colorado. As soon as something better comes along, they'll clear out and I'll be in the money again. I'm betting two weeks tops."

"You always say two weeks. It's never two weeks."

"Whatever. I got my bills paid up and a little scratch to paint the town with. That's all a job's for, right? How about some dinner and a show?"

"Fine. But no movies about Supers." She pulled him closer so he could feel her warmth on his arm. "You always talk all night about what's real and fake in those movies. It's like you're working instead of with me."

"Scout's honor, Delia." He held up two fingers. "You can pick the show. I'm all yours tonight. You can use and abuse me however you want."

"You wish." She gave him a big smile and flipped a dyed red lock of shoulder length hair out of her face. "Although now I think of it, I do have a clogged sink I could *use* you for."

"Tomorrow. Tonight's all good times. How about Italian?"

"Too much like your job. How about Chinese?"

"Don't you start on me, too. Have you been talking to Father Weaver?"

"Yes, but not about you." He felt a pang of jealousy. His joke backfired and he wanted her to talk about him more.

"Well I know you don't have tons of sins to confess. So what's it about?"

"You don't know that. Just because I don't sin with you doesn't mean I don't sin ever. There's more than one kind of sin."

CJ felt his ears grow hot. He was going to have to confess lust again next time. He wished he'd have a lot more to confess, too. He stopped and kneeled down on the sidewalk. "Delia Thompson, will you marry me?"

She looked him in the eyes. "Colin John Leon de la Cruz, no."

He stood up. "How many times do I have to ask? You know I love you. Then it wouldn't be a sin. And we'd save one apartment's rent."

"We've been over this a dozen times. It's not about sex or rent or your job. It's about the lack thereof."

"I'm an independent businessman. Work comes and goes."

She shook her head. "Stand up." He stood. As they walked, she said, "I think you're the best, CJ. But until you can show me something stable, I'm not going to marry you. I just can't live like this forever. I grew up in a hard neighborhood. I don't want my life to be like that anymore. I make enough to get by, but I want the whole fairy tale—house, kids, dog. Anything less and I'm better off on my own."

She stopped walking, put her hands on his shoulders, and turned him to face her. "I can't wait forever. As much as I love you, if you can't figure this out, it won't work out between us. I'm not trying to be manipulative or change you or anything like that. It's just what I need."

CJ looked at her for a long time. Nobody else would understand his job the way Delia did. Yet here she was saying she needed something else. Could he be 'stable' for her? Did he even know how?

"I understand," he said. "All I need is one stroke of luck. One of these Supers is bound to tip the balance of power and stop the infighting. If I'm working for that Super, I'll be set up for life. Can you give me a little time?"

"Sure." She sighed and glanced back down the street at the Bail Bonds shop. "I'm not going anywhere fast. But what makes you think one of them will somehow get control? They've been going back and forth for years."

"I once had a steady job for almost five years, before I met you. Tiger-lady. The outfits were weird, but the money was regular. This is just a temporary condition until things settle down. I'm sure of it." CJ hugged her, taking a moment to smell the lavender in her hair. "I'll work this out. You'll get your fairy tale." She smiled. He didn't have any idea how to make it all happen for her, but she deserved it.

She held him even closer as they walked toward Ming's Chinese Buffet. The sound of a missile streaked overhead, followed by another. Lines of fire arced through the night.

The Supers landed a few blocks to the north.

Delia was already shaking her head when CJ looked at her. "Raincheck? Maybe that's my next job warming up right now."

"How do you know something's wrong? Maybe they are just patrolling or making sure everybody knows they are watching."

"They wouldn't land like that, making big holes in the road, if they didn't have a reason. They are drama-kings."

"Maybe they have a meeting with the mayor and they wanted to show up in style. It looks like they landed near the capital downtown."

"Maybe, but I gotta take leads like this. The only way to find a Super is when they are out in public, fighting or whatever."

She kissed him on the forehead, her brow knit. "Text me when it's all over."

"I can't. I lost my phone."

"Again?!"

"I'll drop by your place after."

"Not after ten. I have work in the morning."

"Maybe I will, too!"

After checking traffic, CJ bolted across the street and raised his hand for a taxi.

8

CJ began to wonder if he'd foolishly left a hot girl for a cold trail. The taxi dropped him in the little park area between the State Capital and the City and County Building. CJ pulled his hoodie up to cover his hat so only the blue bill stuck out the front. He jogged over to the closest tree and crouched low to the ground. He wanted to look like a vagabond.

Supers considered most normals to be beneath them. They saved them from the 'bad guys' whenever they could, but only in a condescending way. They might put their life on the line to save one stranger, but they only connected closely with a few friends and family. Hobos and unwanted sorts were so far below that Supers didn't even see them. Sort of like PETA activists might have a few pets, but they campaigned to save only their favorite animals, ignoring insects, mice, and other unwanted vermin.

It was an unnecessary precaution. Even though Meteoric-man punched him in the face just two days ago, the Super sidekick probably wouldn't remember him at all. CJ didn't blame them or get bitter about it like some people. Most Supers weren't elitist on purpose. They just had a rough job and did the best they could under difficult circumstances. They were just like normals, except on a different level.

CJ jogged across the street and climbed the grass hill toward the capital. The yellow domed building sat like a beacon next to the skyscrapers of downtown Denver. Staying near the trees to one side, CJ had a much better view of the area. He couldn't see the Super duo or their trademark double craters anywhere. He faded into the shadows, leaning against a tall tree trunk, and listened.

If any normal trashed a road, they'd be thrown in jail. If a Super managed to pass themselves off as a hero, like Shooting Star, nobody said anything. If normal cops had to shoot somebody in the line of duty, usually for waving a gun around, everybody got up in arms and protested. If somebody died when a Super was 'saving the world', it was a tragic accident. Just like CJ's father, when The Witch-hunter faced off against Mortal Coil. According to the newspaper, Witch-hunter saved thousands. Nobody said much about the three who died in the crossfire. Sure, two of them were electrocuted by Mortal Coil, but CJ's dad died choking on his own blood with Witch-hunter's crossbow bolt through his chest.

Thou shalt honor they father and mother. He shook his head. He wished Father Weaver hadn't brought it up again. He didn't have time for self-pity right now. He looked at the nearby skyscrapers to see if the Supers had landed on top of them by any chance.

"So you came."

"Aaargh!" When a hand from behind grabbed CJ's arm, his heart almost burst with pounding. CJ turned fast, one hand plunging in to his pocket to grab his Swiss army knife. His knife would be useless in a fight, but having something in his hand made it easier to punch people without breaking fingers. He dropped the weapon. Behind him stood an old woman with long gray hair pulled back into a bun. Bones, tied with leather, made a creepy armor over her chest and arms. Feathers, amethyst crystals, and colored beads decorated the shamanistic outfit. Reddish brown paint—or blood—made a rough glyph on the front of her armor in the shape of a half-closed eye inside a spiral. CJ knew two things. First, she was the new Super in town. Second, this old hag had no chance against SS and MM.

"You just about scared me to death."

"I foresaw your coming here today."

"So? All us lackeys tend to gravitate toward the action." CJ doubted she had any money. He already knew Delia would say she told him so.

"The spirits predicted you would come to me."

"Okay. Are they good spirits? I'm really more about Saints than spirits."

"You will help me."

"Does your power tell you so? Because I tend to need to get paid."

"You will be rewarded. Come with me."

"Right now? Where are we going? You haven't even told me your name or what you want."

"I am Farseer. I come to bring gifts to all those who embrace the way of the spirits."

"Is the gift money?"

"Rest your mind." She put one leathery hand on his forehead, pushing his cap up. Staring into his eyes with her wrinkly gray ones, she whispered a chant. Soon, her raspy words became understandable and light glowed from inside her eyes. "You are in turmoil. You seek to follow the path you believe, against the will of so many others. Your future is split by an axe. My coming will force you down one path and reject the other. You seek the greatness I share. I will set you free."

CJ shivered when she took her icy hand away. She pulled out a wooden club with huge animal teeth protruding from it and handed it to him. He'd been given stranger weapons before. Then she handed him a long straight stick. On closer inspection, it was a tube. Tied around it with a strap of leather were a dozen darts with red pom-poms at the end.

"Are these poisonous?"

"Come with me now." She shuffled off through the shadows of the tall group of trees.

CJ shrugged and did what she said. She might not last long, but if he could get her to pay up front, it might get him by until the next Super arrived. With two opponents in such a short time, Shooting Star probably wouldn't be leaving as soon as he hoped. He seriously doubted this old woman could get rid of SS, but if she kept sneaking around it might last a while.

Farseer led him southwest, within a few blocks of Delia's work, at Sunken Gardens Park. The recreation area was a big triangle with a chunk cut out of it for the First Mennonite Church, leaving a big field to the north and some trees to the south. Farseer led CJ to the trees, finding a copse between the big road and the playground where the grass grew bare because of constant shade. CJ remembered a police officer chasing him out of here once when he was making out with a girl he dated in high school.

The crone lifted a trap door and climbed down a rough wooden ladder. CJ did a double take. One second he'd been sure it was just an empty patch of ground. The next, he stared at a secret entrance. He looked for any kind of camouflage on the door, but found only a roughly framed piece of plywood. He'd been in stranger places, so he climbed down.

At the bottom, he found a large cave lit by candles. More bones, feathers, and glyphs decorated the walls. In some places, the dirt walls had pictographs painted on them. He could make out animals and the spiral-eye, but he had no idea what the wavy lines or choppy slashes might mean.

Two men and a woman were already down there. Sitting on logs making a "V" against two sides of the cave, they all had street clothes like him beneath bead-decorated mantles or leather jerkins. The woman looked young. She had a bit of Gothic flair, like Ana, but didn't look like she always wanted to start a fight. Farseer introduced her as Angel, so they both nodded and grunted greetings.

The shorter man had black hair and light brown skin. He stood up and put out his hand to shake. "I'm George. George Imhoff." His accent sounded Hispanic. A blotchy scar on his left cheek continued down his neck onto his shoulder. There was another pinkish-brown blotch on the other side of his neck, too. He'd had tattoos burned off with a laser recently.

"CJ." He gave a flat smile and tipped the hoodie back so more of his face showed in the dim light.

The other man had lighter brown hair and stayed seated. He flashed a forced smile and lifted one hand to wave. "Jimmy."

Farseer tossed a few pieces of wood into the center of the cave and they flared into a fire without a match. CJ expected the place to fill with smoke, but nothing happened.

When Farseer approached CJ, he asked, "So what brought you to Denver?"

"I had a vision. In it, a black bird told me my destiny lay in this land and I would begin my work here."

"Great. When do we start?"

"You will begin today," the old woman said. "Sit down." She took off his hat and tossed it into the fire."

CJ reached for it too late, gritting his teeth as he ran one hand through his hair to straighten it. He looked at the other three for any clue about what was going to happen.

George said, "It's not that bad."

Farseer stood in front of him so CJ couldn't see anything except the bone armor with the spiral-eye and put her hands on his ears. Were those human bones? She crowed like a bird, then her icy hands grew suddenly warm.

"Spirits, I invoke your favor on this man. I have seen his future, gnarled and divided, on the edge, never fulfilled. Grant him the gift of a forked path. Imbue him with the potential for greatness he stands near but cannot grasp."

Thou shalt have no other gods before me. CJ already knew this wouldn't go over well in confession. His ears tingled, as if the blood in them would burst out. CJ kept quiet, even though his eyes were wide. She let go and moved around behind him.

"Three gates you must pass." She put her warm hands over his nose. CJ found it uncomfortable, and her hands smelled like dirt and strange herbs. "First, you must fight one with a gift and win. Face their power, and come out on top. Only after their gift gives way before you will the spirits recognize your potential and bless you. Only then will you pass the first gate." The heat from her hands made the snot in his nose run. As soon as she moved

them away, he had to snort it back in to keep it from running out. Angel raised one eyebrow and looked away.

She moved her hands to cover his eyes, like a child asking him to "guess who". "The second gate is to see beyond your weakness. See into yourself and recognize the gift. Know and name your gift, and the second gate will be passed." He felt the heat go into his eyes through the eyelids. He didn't like that feeling.

Finally, she moved her hands to his mouth. CJ shut it hard, not willing to taste the strange smelling skin. "The last gate is to taste blood from the gifted. By borrowed blood are the gifts moved to you. This is the third gate. Once you travel through it, your paths will become one and you will be blessed by the spirits until you die."

Farseer moved away, returning with a beaded leather cord. A medallion decorated with small, shiny beads forming her eye logo hung from it. She placed it over his head and hung it around his neck. Then she tied a feather into his hair behind his left ear. She yanked back his hoodie and painted something just below his neck on his back. It tickled.

When she finished, she went to a small rock cubby and brought out jerked beef and nuts. "Let us celebrate. Now we are ready to make our move."

The other three perked up. "About time," Jimmy said. "I can't stand to sit around this place for another day." CJ wondered how long they'd been waiting.

"Any chance we can get paid up front?" CJ asked.

The old woman pulled out four tiny leather bags and tossed one to each of them. CJ frowned as he pulled the gathered top open and poured it into one hand. Small, sparkling rocks tumbled onto his palm. Red, green, and white; a ruby, emerald, and diamond. They all smiled nervously and looked at each other, unsure exactly how much the gems were worth. CJ knew he could fence them, but wondered if he might just be able sell them to a legitimate jeweler.

"You and you"—Farseer pointed to Angel and Jimmy—"will wait at City Park. You two" —she pointed to CJ and George— "will wait at Congress Park. I will draw them out to Chessman Park, then bring them to you."

She traced a rough map in the dirt floor, showing the capital, their current location, and the three other parks. Obviously, she had a thing for parks.

"We're going to take them out with these?" Angel asked, holding up her blowpipe.

"Those, and the water." Farseer grinned wide, revealing stained and missing teeth.

"You think you can take out Shooting Star with water?" CJ asked for clarification.

Farseer bobbed her head up and down, grinning. "I have seen their futures."

9

CJ and George stood on top of the shallow slope of a red-roofed building to the south of the large outdoor pool at Congress Park. The large trees around them blocked most of the city lights, giving them a nice view of the clear sky. A smaller pool to the east meant Shooting Star and his sidekick could come from either of two directions and the plan would still work, theoretically. Climbing up here hadn't been easy. In the early night, the air grew cold.

"So where are you from?" CJ asked George, pushing the feather back behind his ear. It never stopped tickling his ear, no matter where he put it.

"L.A." George, about ten years younger than CJ, scratched his scar idly. In his other hand, he had a switchblade, which he kept flipping open and closed.

"How long you been in Denver?"

"Few weeks. It's been hard to find a job with my, uh, unique abilities. Never expected it would come with some kind of Voodoo ritual."

"It's not Voodoo. I've seen that before. This is something else. Some kind of Shamanism I think." CJ scanned the horizon for any abnormal streaks of light. He noticed a real shooting star and half-smiled. "Whatever it is, I sure didn't sign up for it. She did this weird mind-reading thing and told me a bunch of stuff about my future."

George scoffed. He flipped the knife open and closed again. "You don't believe in that stuff, do you?"

"I don't know. I guess so. I mean, I've seen it all, you know? I've seen magic, *real* magic. I've seen people pray and heal somebody. I've seen who knows how many freaky Supers with every kind of power. One guy called himself The Lobster, and he could morph his hands into all kinds of weird things. Lobster claws were the most normal." CJ laughed, eyeing George's blade. He'd seen a lot of guys with a thing for their knife, so he didn't let the nervous habit bother him.

"Well sure, everybody knows that kind of stuff is real. I mean the thing she did to us. If we pass the three gates, are we going to get some kind of magical powers, too?"

"That would make us Supers." CJ scratched his stubbly chin and flipped the feather behind his ear again. He picked up the medallion Farseer gave him and looked at it. "Every Super has to get their powers somehow. Even supposing she could give people these gifts, why would she?"

"Before you showed up, Jimmy asked her that. She told him she wants to make a whole world full of Supers, one person at a time. But they have to believe in spirits and hate technology." George slipped his knife back in his pocket.

"What's she got against smartphones?"

"I don't know. Something about people not believing. She's like a missionary, trying to get people to believe in the spirits or something."

"I suppose a Super could have the power to make other Supers. I've never seen it before, but that doesn't mean it can't happen." CJ shook his head. "Even if it's true, the list of requirements is pretty steep. Beat a Super, drink blood from a Super. Might as well throw in a millionaire and juggle six chainsaws. Supers come in all shapes and sizes."

"How do you know so much about them?"

"Internet. There are discussion boards, and Superpedia, of course. Most of it is just speculation, but there's a lot of good info if you dig it out."

"I don't think Farseer cares much for the Internet." George lifted off the mantle Farseer had given him and studied it. It looked like leather shoulder pads with more of the strange glyphs from the cave painted on it. "So what about these spirits? Do you believe in those?"

Thou shalt have no other gods before me. "I'm Catholic," CJ said. "I don't think we're supposed to believe in that stuff. Are you religious,

George?"

"My mother was from Argentina. My father from Germany a few generations back." He put the oversized collar back on. "I was christened a Catholic, but then we moved to L.A. and we never went again. I got involved in some gangs there and had to leave town." He pulled the knife back out and began flipping it open and closed again.

"I'm one quarter Spanish," CJ said.

"Doesn't show."

"Is this your first job in Denver? They aren't all like this, you know."

"No. I tried doing collections for a bail bond place."

"Which one?"

He flipped the knife open and left it. "Lucky Break."

A big grin split CJ's face. "No kidding! Then you met Delia. She's my girlfriend."

George nodded and closed the knife. "She's pretty, if you like redheads."

"I do."

"Somebody told me once that they don't have souls."

CJ studied him. Did he really believe that? Was he serious, or just kidding? A light in the sky caught CJ's attention and he pointed. "Looks like the game is on."

The two streaks of fire rose into the air and then turned, gaining speed as they dropped. Just like Farseer predicted, they headed for Chessman Park, only a few blocks to the west.

The sound of them pounding into the dirt echoed and shook the ground.

"What are the odds that two Supers would have the same power like that," George asked, flipping open his knife.

CJ placed a dart in the end of his blowpipe and gripped it tightly. "They don't have the same power, exactly. Shooting Star can blast fire out of his hands. Meteoric-man doesn't take any damage on impact. Somehow, they discovered their powers kind of work together. SS can ignite MM's trail with his fire, and as long as they are close together, SS can smash the ground without getting hurt. It's a rare power symbiosis."

"If they can smash into the ground without damage, are these darts going to work?"

CJ shrugged. The paired streaks of fire rose into the air and came back down for another hit. "It doesn't matter."

"What? Why not?" George looked at CJ as if he'd just spit cockroaches out of his mouth.

"They're Supers. They don't follow the same rules we do. So we don't have to follow their rules. I mean, we'll shoot the darts at them, of course. And we'll hope Farseer wins, because then the paychecks, or little gems, or whatever, will keep coming. But if you get excited about their politics or causes, it just gets you hurt. If you're smart, you'll do what I do. Once you see the game turn against your side, take the fall."

George's eyes went wide as if he were hearing wisdom from a great oracle. CJ enjoyed being taken seriously for once. George said, "So we don't care who wins?"

"We care, because we get paid if Farseer wins. But if you start to play their game, you'll always lose. My last partner, Ana, she just went to jail because she couldn't keep herself emotionally distanced. We're normals. We have to work within our own terms."

George pointed at CJ. "You make a lot of sense."

"Been in this business a long time."

"I'm sticking with you, man."

CJ lifted his toothed club. "Fine, but when they show up, Meteoric-man's mine. You get SS."

"Okay, why?"

"Because sidekicks usually don't hit as hard." CJ felt his jaw, still sore from his last run in with MM. He felt a bit of pride as he thought he was working for somebody good again. Father Weaver would be glad about that, he hoped.

"Look." A bright light flashed in Chessman Park behind the few tall trees of the neighborhood separating them. Then two streaks of fire rose high

THUG #1

into the air again.

"She got away." CJ pointed to the gray-haired woman, standing between the two swimming pools. She made a loud cackling sound, but didn't signal them.

The fire streaks made a wide arc, swerving in a growing spiral as their search radius increased.

"Get down," CJ said softly. He lay on the hard red roofing tiles with his elbows propped over the apex so he faced east. George followed. They could see Farseer hobbling into position between the two pools. When the flying Supers blazed overhead, she put out her hands, holding a stick with feathers tied to it high in the air. A light glowed from her, making it easy for the two Supers to spot her.

They split up, each arching up and around like a sideways figure eight. When they came together, the two raced forward.

They broke the sound barrier as they streaked toward Farseer.

CJ and George shot their darts. CJ had no idea if they even hit their targets. At the last second, Farseer jumped in the Olympic pool. CJ realized her plan. By dropping in the water near the edge, the concrete would act as a barrier against the incoming Supers.

Unable to correct fast enough, the pair plunged in, sending a giant wave up into the air and over the sides of the pool. A great plume of steam began to rise where the water boiled around them.

"Come on," CJ said. He rushed to the lowest corner of the building and dropped down.

George followed. "I thought you said we were done."

"If she's right about the water, we want to be there to look helpful."

CJ walked up. The two Supers had cracked the bottom of the pool. White vapor continued to rise from the chaotic ripples. Farseer, dripping wet, stood with a grin on her face at the edge.

Distant sirens wailed.

Shooting Star, burning like a fire elemental, rose from the pool in a great cloud. He landed on the side of the pool opposite them. Meteoric-man pulled himself up the usual way and climbed out. Farseer's grin disappeared.

"You really thought we'd just die if we hit the water?" Shooting Star said. He looked angry. "I can make enough heat to keep the water from ever touching me."

When MM stood, wringing a small stream from his brown cape, CJ shot him in the chest logo with a blow dart.

George shot one at SS, but he held up his hand and a small stream of fire consumed the tiny projectile. Meteoric-man started to scream. "Piranhas! Don't let them eat me." He rubbed his hands all over his body, trying to wipe away imaginary fish. He fell down, moaning.

"You're going to pay for that!" Shooting Star leaped high into the air, using his flames to push him higher. Halfway across the pool, he turned over and blasted toward the group. George jumped away with a high-pitched yelp. Farseer tumbled back, a look of confusion twisting her dry lips back to show her terrible teeth.

CJ twisted his toothed club hard and hit Shooting Star right in the head.

Fire exploded from the Super as he cried out and then collapsed on the concrete, crashing into a few lawn chairs set up around the pool. His fire went out, leaving a red-clad Super in a heap on the ground. A small trickle of blood flowed from the man's hair.

CJ caught fire. His fingers felt the burning first as it raced up his sleeves. CJ jumped into the pool. Farseer followed him in when her hair went up like a candle.

George helped the other two out. As an afterthought, he shot a blow dart into Shooting Star. The unconscious man began to writhe on the ground, convulsing.

"How did you know that would work?" George asked, incredulous.

"SS only has the fire, remember. MM is the one invulnerable when he crashes into things. Once they're apart, they only have their own power."

George smiled and patted CJ on the back. "Brilliant!"

CJ smiled. "Now let's get out of here."

"You will be rewarded!" Farseer crowed. "You passed the first gate!"

CJ's wet clothes warmed and began to steam. Then his whole body glowed, clothes and all. Red light surrounded him like he'd seen in pictures of saints or angels. His chest felt hot near the medallion, and for a moment, the red light clouded out all his vision.

The warmth slowly dissipated.

"Time to go," CJ said. "We waited too long." He turned to bolt, but the cops already surrounded them.

"Drop your weapons and put your hands up!" the bullhorn blared.

CJ tossed the club and blowpipe. For good measure, he pulled out his Swiss army knife and dumped that, too.

Farseer muttered some kind of curse under her breath. Then she put the stick down. George surrendered his weapons as well.

CJ kneeled down.

"On your knees."

CJ put his hands behind his head.

"Hands behind your head."

The others followed.

"They will not keep me in jail long," Farseer said. "I can see it."

"What about us?" George asked. "I got a record. And I'm Hispanic. I'll never get out of there."

"It will be sooner than CJ," Farseer said.

CJ dropped his head. He'd only been to prison twice before, a small miracle for anybody in this business. The last time the judge said if he got caught working with a Supervillain again, he'd get hard jail time. Farseer was no villain, but cops and judges didn't always see these things properly.

CJ said, "Let's get our story straight and never change it no matter what. We were trying to tell SS and MM to stop breaking up the ground all over Denver. We're environmentalists, get it?"

Thou shalt not bear false witness. Too late for that now.

Farseer nodded. George grunted.

"Silence!"

CJ dropped his head. Delia would leave him after this for sure.

10

The judge threw the book at him. CJ knew it wasn't fair, but that would have to wait for his appeal.

CJ finished two hours of hard exercise. He always worked out when he wasn't on the job, but in jail, there literally was nothing else to do. Daytime television sucked. He watched a soap opera called *Genes*. Normally, the lack of realism in how it depicted Supers bothered him, but he didn't have anything better to do.

Then he watched *Lifestyles of the Super Powered* and a morning replay of *Supertainment Tonight*. He caught these shows to keep up with the mainstream Supers, like most people, but wished they wouldn't always focus on the same two dozen famous Supers. He really wanted more information on the lesser-known Supers. He did pick up a few interesting tidbits about Cliff-hanger, though.

He spent the rest of the morning in his cell thinking about the red glowing thing that happened after he clubbed Shooting Star. Any doubts he once had about Farseer's ritual had vanished. He tried to remember the rest of what she'd said, wishing he hadn't ignored most of it as hokum at the time.

After lunch, CJ settled onto his bunk with a book, *Recovering a Failed Business*. They let him have two at a time from the reading cart. The other was a graphic novel called *Sundown*, but he forced himself to read the boring book first. Business before pleasure. He left the TV on so he could catch the news if they reported anything about Supers.

After a few chapters, he knew this book wouldn't help him. Most of the advice revolved around selling off assets or filing taxes differently. None of it really applied to independent contractors in his line of work. There weren't many resources for people like him.

A brown clad guard rattled the bars. CJ looked up to see the dark skinned man unlocking the door. Without eye contact the guard said, "You have a visitor." Then he walked away.

CJ jumped up, straightening his orange jump suit and rushing to catch the guard. "Who is it?"

The dark skinned guard led him out the next gate and pointed to the short row of desks along a line of wire-enforced glass. Delia sat on the other side.

CJ smiled and grabbed the telephone handset from the wall. "Hello! It's great to see you. You look *amazing*! Thanks for coming." He felt a knot in his stomach, expecting her to end it right then. He hoped an outpouring of positive sentiment might persuade her to stay with him.

"Hello, CJ." She didn't smile, but she didn't look angry, either.

CJ waited, hoping she'd say more. Instead, the even smile on her lips slowly turned down. He said, "I'm so sorry, Delia. I never meant for this to happen. I…"

"Did you really take out Shooting Star?"

He stopped, searching her eyes. Was she angry or impressed? She gave him her best bail-bond-agent face, with no clue about judgment of any kind on her part. He took a deep breath. "Yes. That was me, but it was self-defense. He would have burned us all to a crisp if I didn't."

She nodded. "That's pretty cool. At least you finally did something big." The corners of her red lips curled up.

CJ's jaw dropped. "Thanks."

"So, six years?" Her smile fell again. "That's a long time."

"Yeah. At best, I'll be up for parole in four. I know better than to sit around after a battle like that. But I got caught off guard because Farseer did this weird ritual and told me the spirits would bless me if I passed through three gates. The first gate was to defeat a Super while they were using their powers.

"I didn't really believe it at first, you know. I mean, who'd be dumb enough to take on a Super? But in the moment, I wasn't really thinking about all that. When SS came at us all burning hot, my first instinct was to run. But then, I realized with MM down and all the way across the pool, SS wouldn't be invulnerable. So I just picked up the club and whacked him.

"Even then, I knew to run. But suddenly Farseer's like, 'You will be rewarded.' Then this red glow kind of came out of me everywhere. She said I passed the first gate. I couldn't believe the whole ritual might really work, so I was still there when the cops showed up."

Delia wagged her head. "It was bound to happen sooner or later. Whether you glowed red or got hit by a falling crossbeam or caught in a Super's cape doesn't matter. Sooner or later, you were going to end up back in here. Or worse, you'd end up dead."

"Look, I know you wanted me to get a more stable situation. That's partly why I'm here. I usually stay apart from the Supers and their causes. But this time I thought if I got Farseer positioned well in Denver, and people here saw she is really prophetic and can tell the future, then I might have a long term position and no Supers would show up because everybody here realized she's not a villain. She's a very good person. I really thought this time I could make it work."

"It doesn't matter now." She shrugged.

"I guess not. They never pay independent contractors for jail time." He knew she was going to leave him. He just wanted to keep her here as long as possible. It might be his last visitor for four long years. Lexi wasn't about to let Juliet come see him in prison.

Delia held up the small leather pouch Farseer had given him the day before. He'd sent it to her in a padded mailing envelope. "What about this?"

CJ rolled his eyes. "I can't fence them until I get out. If you could just hold onto them for me, I'm sure they are worth a few hundred bucks at least."

"Six-thousand." Delia put the small bag back in her pocket. "I had them appraised. They're legit."

CJ's jaw dropped. "Wow." He did some quick math in his head.

"Do you want me to sell them?"

"I hoped to just sell two of them and get the diamond made into an engagement ring for you."

She snorted. Whatever else, he counted it a small victory that he broke her cold visage. "I'm not waiting six years, CJ. I'm going to see other men."

CJ resisted the urge to vent his anger. "I can't say I'm surprised. If you're not married when I get out, will you at least date me again? I can get a regular job. I'll do anything to keep you. Please."

A small tear ran down her cheek. "Whatever. We can cross that bridge when we get to it. But I'm not waiting."

"Just do me a favor?"

"What?" Her well made-up eyelids dropped halfway.

"Sell the gems. Give the money to Lexi and tell her it's all I can do for the next few years. Also, tell her the rent went up by fifty dollars."

"Why wouldn't she know the price of her own rent?"

"It's a long story."

Delia took a deep breath. "I'll do it."

"Thanks. I love you. I don't deserve you. If you find somebody stable, I hope he loves you and gives you the babies you want and makes you happy forever."

"That's not what you hope."

CJ winked. "It's my second hope, then."

"Whatever." Delia Thompson hung up the phone and stood. She walked away without looking back. CJ wondered why he couldn't just give her what she wanted and make them both happy. Now, it was probably too late.

Since there were only a few things to do in the slammer, CJ signed up for all of them. One was Sunday Mass, of course. *Thou shalt honor the sabbath day to keep it holy.* He waited with a handful of orange clad inmates in a stark gray concrete room on a metal bench. All the religions used this same chapel, so there were several different symbols in the front of the room next to the podium. They didn't have a proper crucifix, so the priest settled for a plain cross.

When the preacher finally came in, CJ was thrilled to see Father Weaver. He let a smile cross his face, despite the less than approving glance of his spiritual leader. At least his friend smiled when he took the sacrament.

After mass, Father Weaver stayed for confession. Half the men left. The others went in one at a time. CJ waited, signaling each time for the others to go before him. The last one, a younger Hispanic man with gang tattoos on his wrists and hands, took a long time. CJ wondered what he could have done to take so long.

At last, CJ went to the small confessional. It was just a concrete box with a thick wire mesh screened hole between him and the priest. There wasn't even a bench to sit on.

CJ hunched over, so his mouth would be closer to the screen when Father Weaver said, "Bless you my child."

"It's me, CJ."

The shadowy image nodded behind the screen.

"It's been two weeks since my last confession. I broke the law. I hit Shooting Star in the head with a club. He was on fire, though, coming straight at the three of us, including a very old woman. We hadn't broken any laws or anything. He just attacked us without any evidence of a crime of any kind."

"What else?"

CJ let his voice trail off. He had a lot more justifications he'd hoped to tack on. "Lust I guess. But she kind of dumped me. I suppose I covet getting out of here. But since I'm stuck for several years, that's probably not going away any time soon."

"Is that all?"

"Yes."

"Forty Hail Marys and forty Prayers to Joseph. I want you to do Evening Prayer every night for as long as you are in here, too."

"Okay." Mentally, CJ scolded himself. He still hadn't done the thousand prayers he'd been assigned last time. He'd have plenty of time now, but he wondered if failing to say them soon enough is what landed him in jail, some kind of holy payback.

He decided to confess that, too.

"It's okay." Father Weaver took a deep breath. "So what happened, CJ?"

CJ told the whole story again. When he mentioned Farseer's ritual, the priest stopped him. "What? Tell me everything about it."

CJ related the story about the three gates and how he glowed red after taking down Shooting Star. "If I'd just run instead, as I knew I ought to, I wouldn't be here now. God's probably punishing me for not saying my repentance prayers fast enough."

"I don't think it works like that. CJ, I don't like this Farseer. The Bible is very specific about sorcerers and peeping wizards. They are from Satan."

"She doesn't seem like she's Satanic. I've known a few of those in my time. She's more American Indian type. She speaks of powers as gifts from some invisible spirits."

"The only good spirit is the Holy Spirit of God. You'd do better to stay away from this woman."

"Won't be hard now." CJ laughed sardonically. "Anyway, I saw on the news that she got out already. We didn't really do anything wrong, and they didn't want to give an old lady with no priors a long sentence."

"Hopefully she'll be gone soon."

"I don't know. She said she planned to make a lot of people into Supers, or something along those lines. Unless another Super shows up, she'll probably stick around now that SS and MM are out of the way."

"CJ, listen to me. I fear if you complete this pagan ritual, you will lose your soul. This is the great temptation of your life, your fruit in the Garden of Eden."

CJ thought of Delia. This garden would be a lot more fun if he had an Eve. "Don't worry," CJ said. "I probably won't see her again. Plus, she's *really* old. She probably won't even live until I get out."

Father Weaver made the sign of the cross. "Go and sin no more."

CJ smiled, but he kept the laugh in.

11

few days later, during CJ's workout, the same guard interrupted him by jangling the keys in the metal door lock. CJ looked through the bars and said, "Another visitor?"

"Nope."

CJ followed the cryptic guard anyway. It's not like he had anything else to do.

When they left the main area, the guard held open a wooden door with a heavy metal lock. "Here." He indicated with his other hand for CJ to go in. Sitting on the far side of a wooden table was a woman wearing a badge.

"Hello, CJ. I'm Detective Barton. I'd like to ask you a few questions."

"Then you need to get my lawyer in here. I already answered all the questions before the trial."

"I have different questions. Please, sit down."

CJ scanned her face. Early parole depended on good behavior. He shrugged and sat, looking straight at her. She had green eyes and brown hair with a bit of red in it, touched by just a little make-up, probably just enough to not draw comments from her cop-friends. He gave a fake smile. "What do you want to know?"

"I'm working with a special unit, investigating Super-human and paranormal phenomena. We've been tracking a woman named Alameda Young. Do you know her?"

"No. Sorry."

"Sometimes she calls herself Farseer."

"Ah." CJ nodded and looked to the side. This conversation was over. In his business, even the slightest hint of loose lips and you would never get a job again.

"Court records indicate you were with her and some of her gang on the day you were arrested."

"Yes, I was with her that day. She doesn't have a gang, though."

"What can you tell me about her?"

"She's old and looks frail, but she has a lot of inner beauty."

"What about her powers?"

"I don't know what you're talking about."

The woman's jaw tightened, then she gave a hint of a smile. "Some of the people working with you and her claim she has the gift of foresight. She can predict the future."

"If she can predict the future, why didn't she know the cops were coming and keep us from getting arrested?" CJ tipped his head to the side and opened his eyes wide. "If she has this gift you speak of, wouldn't she have avoided Shooting Star and Meteoric Man altogether?"

"I don't know," Detective Barton said. "Maybe it only works some-times."

"I wish I could tell you I saw it work. If I did, I would have gotten some horse names from her and made a pile of money at the races."

"But she did have a lot of money, in the form of valuable gems, right?"

CJ shook his head. He wasn't denying the statement; he was just sur-prised the others had given her up so easily. He guessed it was Jimmy. George had invested too much in the business and Angel looked like she had authority issues. "I don't know. What do you mean by, 'a lot'? I didn't see anything that made me believe she was rolling in it."

The detective stood, trying to look casual as she paced around, but CJ sensed her anger bubbling just below the stone visage. She even glanced at the one-way mirror, a sure sign somebody watched this interview. "You know, I have a lot of sway with the parole boards. If you cooperate with me, your stay here could be much shorter."

Shorter stay on planet earth, too. CJ snorted. "Believe me, if I had any-thing useful, I would tell you. Like I told the judge, I got involved with

Farseer because we both care about the environment. Shooting Star and his sidekick were wreaking havoc all over Denver. Every time those so-called heroes decided to make a grand entrance, they did fifty thousand dollars in damage to the roads. I was stuck in traffic for hours because of it. And when they land in parks, it's worse. They kill trees by messing up their roots. We don't need that kind of wanton destruction here."

"Have you ever been involved with any other environmental activist groups in the past?"

CJ closed one eye and thought. "Uh, sure. I worked with Animanimal for a short time to try to protect local endangered species from humans destroying their environment."

"You really expect me to believe you were working with villains because you love nature?"

"Farseer isn't a villain. Shooting Star attacked us without provocation. We didn't break any laws or hurt anybody."

"That's not how the jury saw it."

CJ clenched his jaw. "Just tack the title Superhero on anybody's name and everything they do is good, right?"

Detective Barton scoffed. "Clearly you are not in the mood to cooperate. That's not going to look good to your parole board."

"Do you think every time a cop kills somebody in the line of duty it's justified?"

"Mr. Cruz, this interview isn't about what I think."

"You think we should give all police officers a license to kill anybody they want?"

"Of course not. That's absurd."

"Why not? Wouldn't you like a little more edge over the dirt bags you deal with every day?"

"Some of them, yes." She looked straight at him without blinking. "But it would be too easy to abuse."

"Maybe some cops wouldn't think about the consequences before they pull the trigger?"

"Maybe." She seemed bored now.

"How is that different from these so-called heroes? They aren't held accountable for property damage. Nobody makes them answer for their crimes."

"If they commit crimes they are villains."

"Really? So if Shooting Star destroys a public road, it's not a crime? What if I do it? Or you?"

"You're not protecting the city."

"Neither was he. Can you tell me one illegal thing Farseer did? Or me? What did we do to justify being attacked by the streaking duo?" CJ heard a muffled laugh behind the one-way glass, but he didn't break his concentration.

"Trespassing. Besides, you were working for a Supervillain." Detective Barton smacked her hand down on the table.

"Trespassing? That's a two-hundred-dollar misdemeanor. You think I deserve six years in jail for trespassing?"

"You were under court order to stop all contact with villains after your last arrest." She pulled open a manila envelope and scanned the file.

She impressed CJ by knowing it so well. "How am I supposed to know she's a 'villain'? She didn't have a sign saying she was a villain. She's not listed in the Supervillain registry. And she never broke the law or did anything wrong. How could I possibly know?"

"You hit Shooting Star in the head with a toothed club!" Barton slammed the file closed. "You attacked a defender of the city."

"It was self-defense! He attacked us! And I didn't know of any legal status making him special. Where is the registry of city defenders I can look at so I know when my right to self-defense is negated? Where's the list of so-called heroes and villains I can look at to know when my rights no longer exist?"

"Everybody knows—"

"No!" CJ stood and smacked the table. "I didn't do anything wrong. If you want to find the real villains in this situation, go interview Shooting Star."

"We can't. He's been moved to a secure hospital in Detroit. Apparently, he never recovered from whatever hallucinatory drugs your friend George shot him with. Luckily Meteoric-Man recovered from the one you shot him with."

CJ shrugged and sat down. "Self-defense. The crazy guy was going to burn us all to char. And if he did, none of you would have done *anything* about it. It would just be regrettable collateral damage in the line of saving everybody. Well news flash, I have the right to protect myself from becoming collateral damage. If you can't see that, you don't deserve to be a cop at all."

The detective looked at CJ for a long time. He turned away and pretended to be interested in something on the table. Without another word, she stood and left him alone in the room. CJ indicated the mirrored glass by pointing accusingly. "Protect and serve. Isn't that what you're supposed to do? Well, when are you going to protect me? Where were you when a man in stretchy pajamas threatened to cremate me alive?"

No response, of course. A minute later, the door opened again and the enigmatic guard signaled with his dark skinned hand for CJ to follow him out.

I'm never getting out of here. I hope that lawyer wasn't lying when he said we had good grounds for an appeal.

CJ stalled at the doorway, watching if anybody would come out of the observation room.

"Move," the guard said.

As he turned to follow the uniform, the red fletching of a dart stuck out of the guard's neck. The large man tipped and collapsed to the ground.

George and Farseer stood by the front entrance to the prison. George, wearing a similar orange jump suit, motioned with the blowpipe. "Come on!"

CJ sprinted up the hall. By the time he reached them, they were already out the front and into daylight. Two more guards were lying on the ground.

He followed the old woman to an old, green jeep. He jumped in as George gunned it, and the car lurched forward.

As they left the long road between the outer fence and the main prison building, alarms went off. The twelve-foot high chain-link gate with razor wire across the top closed automatically behind them.

They sped along the frontage road going so fast CJ expected they might flip. When they reached the freeway entrance, George signaled right for the first onramp. Farseer closed her eyes and said, "No, go left."

They waited for the light, went under the overpass, and entered the freeway going north. Helicopters chopped the afternoon air behind them. Farseer pointed to the first exit.

Police sirens wailed in every direction. CJ clenched his jaw. This old woman was going to get another twenty years tacked onto his sentence. Why hadn't he just stayed put and waited for the appeal?

"There." Farseer pointed to a strip mall parking lot. She gave him directions to park in a specific spot. "Leave the keys."

They all jumped out and followed her into a store labeled Panaderia. George, like CJ, kept whipping his head around in every direction. The sirens seemed to be everywhere, but they never saw one cop car.

When they went in the small shop, Farseer pointed to the bathroom. The two men went in and closed the door. CJ stared at George who just shrugged. There wasn't much space in the smelly, tiled room.

Two minutes later, Farseer opened the door and tossed CJ a pile of fabric. She closed the door behind her and left him to sort it. Lifting one piece after another, CJ realized they were clothes. Soon they both had on striped Mexican ponchos over denim jeans and white t-shirts.

"This isn't very inconspicuous," George said, tossing the orange jumpsuit aside.

"No. It's genius." He put toilet paper over their balled up prison attire in the nearly full garbage can. "Nobody would expect us to wear rainbow colors if we're hiding."

They went back out to the shop to find Farseer talking with a woman almost her age across the counter.

"You have proven yourselves to be loyal," Farseer said to them.

CJ's eyes went wide. He whispered, "Not in front of—" He pointed to the shopkeeper.

She gave him a gnarly-toothed grin. "She can't speak English."

"But she can identify us," George said.

"We'll be gone." Farseer handed each of them a piece of bread with a swirl of cinnamon that almost matched the spiral-eye on her bone shirt. She held CJ's hand a moment longer and said to him, "You are my general, my right-hand man. You passed the first gate and resisted the interrogator. CJ, you will be my number one."

Farseer motioned for them to follow and headed out the door. George clapped CJ on the shoulder. "That's pretty cool, right?"

CJ shook his head. "Or it's a death sentence when the next Super shows up."

The helicopters and police cars danced around them, but Farseer kept them just out of sight, leading them down strange roads and back alleys on foot. After a few minutes, CJ and George didn't even question. They went when she went and stopped when she stopped. They hid in shadows, they doubled back often, and they sprinted across streets. Eventually they lifted the lid on the hidden lair and descended the ladder.

Farseer slumped in a wicker chair, thoroughly exhausted. She pointed at a cooler and then wiggled her finger at CJ and George. CJ popped the top and George took out a bottle of juice and another of water. He held them up and Farseer pointed to the water. He twisted the cap off for her and she nursed it.

CJ grabbed a bottle of apple juice and tapped it against George's before they tipped them both up and took long swallows. When they caught their breath and finished their drinks, Farseer sat up. Her gray hair stuck out in odd places even more than usual. She pointed at CJ and held her finger out for a long time. CJ glanced at George who shrugged just a little.

"You will be my number one," she said. "The spirits will honor you first."

"My gift?" CJ asked.

She squinted and nodded as if she were seeing his future as they spoke. It made CJ uncomfortable. He tried not to recall what Father Weaver had said about all this. "It will happen. We will make it happen. Then everybody will know."

"Do you know what my gift is?"

"The second gate. No way to know until you pass the second gate." She tipped her head to the side, and closed her eyes. A few seconds later, she started snoring.

George made a quiet laugh and sat on one of the logs.

CJ looked around. The single room didn't have a television or computer, only a small shelf with a few old books. CJ thumbed through a couple, seeing they were mostly hand drawn pictures and not in English. He whispered, "What are we supposed to do now?"

George whispered back, "There's not really anything *to* do. Just sit, I guess."

"And this is better than prison how?"

"The food's definitely worse." He tossed CJ a granola bar. "But the money's good."

CJ eyed the ladder longingly. Without a radio, they wouldn't even know when the cops finally called off the manhunt.

ALTHOUGH IT WAS PROBABLY ONLY A FEW HOURS, CJ COULD HAVE SWORN THE old woman slept for a whole day. He chatted with George until even that grew boring.

When she woke, her eyes were wild. "You must go on a scouting mission."

"Both of us?" George's voice didn't hide his desperation to get out.

"Yes."

"What are we scouting for?"

"The spirits have felt a new gifted one searching for me."

CJ bobbed his head. "A new Super in town already?"

"That's fast?" George asked.

"Yeah, that's too fast. Maybe they sent somebody from the Control Crew."

"Those guys in New York?"

"They don't only work in New York." CJ held out his hands. "That's just their headquarters. They go all over the world, wherever there's a big enough need."

Farseer stared at the ceiling. "There is only one."

"Sometimes they do solo missions, but I don't think we are a big enough threat to rate a member of the Control Crew. Even Shooting Star and Meteoric-man are small potatoes compared to those guys."

Farseer tossed the colored poncho back to George. She handed a black button-down shirt to CJ. "Stay hidden."

George said, "Really, I have to wear this because I'm Mexican? Don't you think that's just a little bit racist?"

"Which direction should we go?" CJ asked.

"Follow the river." Farseer shook her hands and looked around.

"The Platte? Should we go up or downstream?" CJ tried to see whatever drew the old woman's attention.

Farseer, lost in her own thoughts, didn't even register their voices. The pair wasted no time getting up the ladder into the fresh night air. CJ felt a rush as the idea of being free filled him. Then he squelched it. The first cop to make their identities would be the end of his freedom for the rest of his useful life.

George must have had the same thought. "If we were smart, we'd get out of town."

CJ patted his companion's shoulder. "If we were smart, we'd have nine-to-five jobs with chubby wives and a bunch of kids."

They stayed in the shadows of the trees surrounding Sunken Gardens Park, cautiously watching the road to the east as they approached.

"You think she means Cherry Creek?" CJ asked.

"That's the only thing around here like a river," George said. "It's between two big roads, though. We'll be easy to spot."

"Not necessarily," CJ said, rubbing the five o'clock shadow around the two moles on his cheek. "The lights from the cars don't really show much detail below the road. There's a jogging path that runs the length of it, with enough bridges we should be able to take cover if necessary."

CJ sprinted across the three-lane street when traffic paused. George joined him in the shadow of trees on the other side. They made their way down the rocks to the paved path. It wasn't as hidden as CJ would have liked.

"Should we run?" George asked.

"I think we should act casual. Just two guys out for a nice stroll, you know?"

"Which way?"

CJ looked up and down the long line of water. "Follow the river." He spoke his thoughts aloud. "Downstream, I suppose. That seems more like following it than upstream, don't you think?"

"WHAT ARE WE SUPPOSED TO BE LOOKING FOR AGAIN?" GEORGE ASKED AFTER they reached the junction where Cherry Creek joined the South Platte at Confluence Park.

CJ looked away from a pair of teens rolling around on the grass. "A Super. I get the feeling that's all she knows. Apparently, spirits like to talk in riddles. I'm not sure I even believe in such things."

"My mother did." George kept reaching into his pocket for his knife out of habit. They'd confiscated it at the prison, though, so he didn't have it anymore.

"I thought your mother was Catholic."

"Of course, but that doesn't mean she didn't believe in spirits. She didn't talk about it a lot, but she knew when things would bring bad luck."

They followed the curved walks through the park and then continued along next to the bigger river, still going downstream. "Father Weaver says all that kind of stuff is from the devil."

"I don't think so," George said. "I think there's good and bad spirits, same as there's good and bad angels."

"Bad angels?"

"Like demons and devils."

"Ah." CJ kicked a pebble into the slow moving water. "Do you think all that stuff is related to Supers somehow?"

"I don't know, man. How long do we have to go?"

CJ took a deep breath. "I figure we go for another two hours. If we haven't seen anything, we head back. We get back before dawn, then we can sleep half the day and have less staring-at-the-walls time."

"Makes sense. How will we know if we see a Super? Couldn't it just be somebody walking on the side of the road? We might go right past them and never know."

"True. Thing is, this one showed up fast. That means it's somebody serious, probably somebody we've heard of. Those types always have fancy costumes and make a big show out of everything. Nobody would spend the big bucks to hire a mercenary Super to go after Farseer. I think we'll know it when we see it."

"That old woman's premonitions are usually good."

"Anybody who can do a jailbreak without ever seeing a cop? Yeah, she's pretty good."

They went under the freeway and a few more bridges. When they came to the next freeway overpass, a commotion to the east caught their attention. Bright lights were on in the middle of the night. He followed the trail of the unusual activity. Staying on the far side of the street, they worked their way across a giant parking lot beneath the freeway. They kept to the shadow of the big road, pausing at concrete pillars. Another train depot lay farther down the street, but he stopped across from the National Western Stock Show. The tall building held a giant amphitheater for rodeos.

In the parking lot, a cowboy reared back on his brown horse. He had the iconic hat, boots, holstered guns, and badge pinned to a leather vest of a classic Western Sheriff. Another man in plaid with a different silver badge sat atop a white horse nearby. Reporters and a few spectators willing to be out this late at night surrounded the mounted duo.

CJ jerked away, his back pressed against the column. He pulled George back next to him.

"What is it?"

CJ shook his head. "That's our Super."

"The desperadoes? How could you tell from here? One of them is wearing tennis shoes and a baseball cap."

"That's Deputy Knight, the sidekick."

"Sidekick? Farseer said there was only one Super."

"Technically that's true. Deputy Knight doesn't have a super power really. He just finds jobs and does the paperwork."

"Paperwork? Who's the one with the big mustachio?"

"This is much worse than I realized. After Shooting Star, I figured Farseer could handle almost anybody. I didn't think about him."

George peeked around the corner again. "There are news cameras. Wouldn't they want to do this during primetime instead of the middle of the night?"

"That's just it." CJ looked once more to be sure, then he grabbed George and rushed back the way they'd come. Only when they were back on the hiking path next to the river, did he finish the conversation. "That guy doesn't do anything the right way. He's completely unpredictable."

"A Superhero that doesn't follow rules?" George glanced over his shoulder at the night. "That's a villain, right?"

"Deputy Knight keeps him in line. Most people think they're heroes, but it's the one guy Farseer won't be able to get ahead of."

"What's his name already?"

"Random Acts of Cowboy. Most people just call him Rack."

13

For the sixth time, Farseer said, "I have seen his future."

CJ slapped his forehead with his hand. "You can't see his future. That's the whole reason they call him Random Acts of Cowboy. He never does what anybody expects."

"The spirits have told me he will be on Main Street at high noon." Farseer looked pleased with herself.

CJ took a deep breath. He knew they were playing into Rack's hands. Taking a cowboy on in a duel was the worst possible strategy. It was a cliché. But, what else could he do? He wasn't in charge, and she was the one who could see the future. "Denver has a Main Street? I've never been on it."

Farseer pointed to a map. "Here."

"That's in Alameda, by the federal building." CJ scratched his chin. After a few days, he definitely needed a shave. "At least let us get some real weapons. He's a fast draw, and he won't hesitate to pull the trigger, unlike cops."

George held up his blowpipe. "He could shoot us three times before we got one of these darts out, and from a lot farther than these can go." He rubbed the tattoo scar on the side of his face.

"Then you will pass the first gate," she said.

"You could be the new number one," CJ suggested to George.

"No." Farseer reached an arthritic hand out and placed it on CJ's chest.

"You will cross the second gate."

"Great. I hope my power is being bullet proof," CJ mumbled.

Before they left, Farseer dug out another beaded medallion and some bits of feather and leather for each of them. She gave them each new weapons.

CJ studied his. It was a club with an animal skull on the end and two sharp horns. The horns didn't match the skull. He gave it a few test swipes. It was an awkward club. He tried thrusting with it like a pitchfork. Several of Farseer's guests watched him with veiled amusement. It definitely didn't make him feel confident.

"I miss my knife," George said.

CJ patted his shoulder and turned to Farseer. "Me, too. We can stop at a store on the way."

They climbed up to the park above. Over the next hour, dozens of people walked up to Farseer. She did the ears, nose, eyes, mouth ritual with each one.

"Where did these people come from?" George asked CJ out the side of his mouth.

CJ shrugged. He kept his eyes open for Rack. "No way people aren't going to notice this."

NORTH OF A HUGE COLLECTING FIELD OF SOLAR PANELS, THEY FOUND A PARK-LIKE area with grass and trees on both sides of Main Avenue. CJ wasn't surprised at all when Farseer decided this was where they'd wait. At least they had burritos for lunch. It was always better to face a Super on a full stomach.

"If that was my last meal as a free man," George said, "at least it was a good one. Hey, do you think one of these darts could take out a horse?"

CJ fiddled with the horns on his club, trying to decide if the leather straps would break when he smacked it against somebody's head. "I don't know. One sent SS to the mental ward, so they might be strong enough to freak out a horse. That's a good strategy, by the way. Let's use that for our opener."

As they chatted, another two-dozen people came and went. Farseer ritually inducted each one to the, "path of three gates," as she called the process of becoming a Super.

"These people all going to work for Farseer?"

CJ smiled at a young mother who held up her baby as Farseer did the glowy-eyed chant. "I don't think so. I think they are all just hoping to become Supers."

"How'd they all find out about her?" George put down the blowpipe.

CJ shrugged. "She definitely didn't advertise on the internet. Maybe they said something about it on the news while we were in jail. I don't know if they are spreading the word through Twitter or Facebook or what, but it's a good bet the cops are going to find us here soon."

"Assuming Rack doesn't find us first?"

"Right."

"What happens if all these people become Supers?" George shook hands with a particularly enthusiastic teenaged boy.

CJ smiled. "I like the idea of more people becoming Supers. Too few people have had all the power for too long."

George tipped his head sideways. "So Farseer really has two powers. She can see the future *and* make people Supers."

CJ fiddled with his new beaded medallion. This one just had a sunburst over a mountain. Apparently, Farseer ran out of the stuff with her logo on it. "Most Supers have more than one power. They tend to go in pairs. That's the most common. They often complement each other, but it's not required. Some Supers have a bunch of powers, while others have one power that's just really strong. There's a whole level system people use to rate them. You can look it up on Superpedia."

"Farseer hates phones, remember?"

"Look it up later, then. The Control Crew won't let anybody in lower than level four. So they have to have at least four powers, or one power that's four times stronger than other Supers with that power."

"Shooting Star flies and shoots fire, but Meteroic-man just did the crash into the ground without getting hurt thing." George took out his new knife and began flipping it open and closed.

"MM probably had the symbiosis power that let the two of them use both of their powers." Most of the hopeful Supers steered clear of them when George had the knife out.

One man didn't seem to care. Slightly overweight and a little shorter than George, he walked right up to them. "So she's the one they say can give people Super powers?"

CJ shook the man's hand. Until Rack or the police showed up, he might as well do something to help out. "Yes. It's a little more complicated than that, but you can get the gist of it from the ritual." The man kept looking around at the buildings like a tourist, so CJ added, "You're not from around here?"

"I live in Salt Lake City." He handed CJ a business card. "But when I heard about all this, I took a personal day and drove out here. This is too good to pass up, right. Is it true? Does it really work?"

George put the knife away and stood up to join the conversation. "Sure it works, but you got to do your part."

The man noticed the last person was done and walking away, so he thanked them and walked over to Farseer. She put her hands on his ears and started the chanting without any introduction.

"What if she changes the whole world?" George said. "Imagine a world where every single person is a Super."

CJ patted George's shoulder. "I like that world." He looked at the card in his hand. *Travis Mueller. Robotics and Electrical Engineering.*

"Are you kidding? It would be crazy."

"Only at first. Then people would sort things out and life would go on. People would still need food and want to fall in love. It's not like Supers are that different from normals."

"I don't know, man." George turned when the man made a sudden move.

"Stop!" He grabbed Farseer's wrists and pulled her hands away from his mouth.

CJ jumped toward them, inserting his skull staff between them in order to protect Farseer from anything the man might try.

"Step back," CJ said.

"I'm not going to hurt her." Travis put his hands up.

Farseer tipped her head to the side. "Now I look into the future and tell you the path."

"Not me," the man said. "I don't want that part." His head began to glow red, then the light spread over his body. A moment later, it went out.

"He has passed the first gate." Farseer squinted her eyes, giving a tight smile at the same time.

"Whoa!" George picked up his blowpipe. "That's new."

"Thank you," Travis said. He had a satisfied expression on his face, as one whose plan had come to fruition. He stepped further away.

"Any chance you guys know where I can find another Super?"

CJ opened his mouth to answer, but closed it.

"Random Acts of..." George started, but CJ put a hand up to stop him.

"Why do you ask?" CJ inserted his body physically between Travis and Farseer, holding the club cross-wise in two hands.

"The second gate. She said the first gate was to stop a Super using their power, so I stopped her from telling my future. The next gate is to find my powers. But I need a Super for that."

CJ's long experience working around Supers made him cringe at this guy's naiveté. "You get full marks for enthusiasm, but you might want to take it easy. Some Supers are dangerous."

"Thanks for the tip." Travis waved at them all kindly and walked away. As he did, the sound of horse hooves clomping along the side of the road grew steadily louder.

"Here we go," George said. He ran to the closest tree and leaned against it, his loaded blowpipe resting across a low branch.

Farseer gave her wide, toothless grin. "I have seen into his future. He will fall from his saddle."

All the would-be Supers scattered. Finished with Farseer, they didn't want to be guilty by association. A few cars driving by pulled over to watch.

The horses sauntered into view, Rack in front and Deputy Knight bringing up the rear. Beneath his thick moustache, Rack gave a smile. He reached up and tipped his tan hat. "Good mornin', ma'am." Rack put the reins down on the pommel of the saddle and crossed his hands over it so he could lean down and talk, as if this were polite conversation. "My partner and I, we'd like to ask you a few questions."

"You will fall!" Farseer screeched, raising her rune stick. CJ flinched when she yelled in his ear.

Rack pulled out a long, shiny silver gun and checked the bullets as he spun the revolver cylinder.

Travis ran up to Rack. The Super pointed the gun at the man, then seeing his empty hands, lifted it toward the sky. "You need to step back, little man, before you get hurt."

Rack pulled the reins and his horse turned in a circle. Deputy Knight put up his cell phone, taking a picture of Travis. "He's a programmer. No criminal record. He's a civilian, but for the Air Force on drones."

"Actually, I can build anything." Travis said. Then the red light washed over him again.

"What the..." Rack pulled both guns and pointed them at Travis.

When the light faded, Travis called up, "That's two!"

George and CJ looked at each other, eyes wide.

"You're going to shoot an unarmed man?" Travis asked, raising both his hands.

Rack holstered one of his guns. "What just happened to you?"

"I can tell you," Travis said, lowering his hands so he could signal for the cowboy to come closer, "but it's a secret."

Rack's horse reared up and Travis jumped back. Rack fired once into the

air. He calmed the horse and moved closer, leaning down. Travis punched the man right in the nose. Then he fell to the ground and covered his head with both hands.

Rack fell out of the saddle. As a small trickle of red came down from the Super's nose, Travis glowed red again.

"The third gate!" Farseer crowed.

Rack had his gun pointing at Travis in less than a second. "You're under arrest."

Travis put up his hands and stood. "I'll go quietly."

"Why'd you hit me?" Rack was shaking with anger. "And why do you keep glowing?"

Travis shrugged. "I just wanted to see what would happen. You know, just a random idea."

Rack scrunched up his forehead for a moment, then he leaned back and laughed.

"That's a good one. It's refreshing to see somebody who understands me. Deputy, cuff him."

Deputy Knight dismounted and came forward with handcuffs.

Rack raised his gun to point at Farseer, who was still standing behind CJ.

"You, too. All of you."

Rack slapped his hand up to his neck, pulling out the dart.

He fired twice at George. Both bullets tore huge chunks of bark from the tree George hid behind. A faint red light emanated from behind the tree.

George said, "Yes!"

When Rack pulled the other gun, so he could cover both George and Farseer, CJ felt his ears grow hot and his vision tint red. As Rack moved his guns to cover George, Farseer, and Travis in turns, CJ knew Rack's power wasn't just unpredictable behavior. This was also a lucky cowboy, so his seemingly irregular actions always worked. The only way to beat such a man would be a plan where there was no chance of failure or escape. At the same time, CJ noticed a taxi driver parked in the shade of a nearby tree with the engine running.

"The first gate," Farseer said, pointing at George with her stick. She slapped CJ on the back. "The second gate." Each time she spoke of somebody passing a gate, her aged voice resonated with sheer bliss.

"I swear I'm going to shoot the next person to glow with red light." Rack waved his guns at everybody he could see. "What's happening?"

Deputy Knight turned away from Travis before cuffing him and held up his phone. "Based on the old woman's file, I'd say they are all becoming

Supers."

"What?" Rack's hands shook. "Supervillains everywhere?"

"Not villains," CJ said. He lifted the club to speak, but Rack trained both barrels on him, so he dropped the stick and held his hands up. The venom on this dart was taking much longer than it did on Shooting Star. "Just Supers. They could be heroes or villains, or neither."

"Shut-up!" Rack yelled.

Rack fired into the air. "Next person who talks gets a stomach full of lead.

"Everybody just stay where you are and put your hands where I can see them." Most of the people in the area were already complying. "You, behind the tree, get out here where I can see you. Join them others."

George moved out slowly, hands in the air. He walked over by CJ and Farseer. Rack wiped his nose on his sleeve. The sight of his own blood just served to irritate him further.

"Cuff 'em all," Rack ordered. "We'll sort them out at the station."

"How will you get all of us to the station?" Travis asked. "It's miles away and you're on horseback."

"On it," Deputy Knight said. He put the phone to his ear. "We need several police cars on Main Street." He paused. "Main Avenue, whatever, yes." He lowered it. "Two minutes, Rack."

"Why isn't he all crazy and crying on the ground?" George whispered.

CJ whispered back, "One of his powers is luck. The dart probably hit him in a way it didn't get the toxin into his bloodstream."

"How do you know that?"

CJ shrugged. "It's my job. Same way I know the only chance of getting out of this is to get Farseer into that taxi." He tipped his head.

George said, "How?"

"We just need a diversion."

Travis dropped his hands. "I'm leaving. If you're going to stop me, you'll have to shoot me in the back." The man turned and half-jogged toward the solar panels.

Rack lifted the gun to shoot him.

"No," Deputy Knight said. Rack nodded, holstered the guns, and ran after Travis.

"Now," CJ whispered.

George punched Deputy Knight in the face.

They each took one of Farseer's arms and ran, almost carrying her, to the taxi.

"Rack!" Deputy Knight called as the trio tucked into the back seat.

"Drive!" CJ yelled at the driver.

Shocked, the man put his foot down and the car launched forward.

"Stop!" Rack hollered.

Bullets shattered the window on CJ's side of the car. Pain lanced through his chest before he blacked out.

14

When CJ woke, diffuse lights in strange places confused him. He had a needle in his arm with a clear tube coming out of it, and another tube coming out of his chest. A machine, beeping in rhythm, began to beep faster.

His back ached on the left side. When he moved his arm, it screamed pain at him. He closed his eyes, realizing he was dizzy from medication. He was in a hospital.

When the hurt subsided, he ventured to open his eyes again and see what was around him. The door let in most of the light. To the other side someone with wild red hair lay under a blanket on a folding cot.

Delia. He wanted to hug her, but knew he couldn't move, so he just whispered her name.

Soon she sat up, blood-shot eyes full of hope. "CJ! You're awake!" She pushed the blanket aside and leaned over, kissing him on his dry lips.

"Good to see you," he said with a raspy voice.

She put a straw to his lips and he sucked some warm water that tasted like plastic. "The doctors were worried for a while, but they said you finally stabilized around midnight."

"What happened?" CJ had vague memories of George and Rack.

"You were shot. They just took you off the ventilator." She glanced at the door and back to him. "George gave them a fake name for you. I think he pickpocketed somebody's wallet and used their insurance card. He said it wouldn't be long before they figured it out and came back to arrest you."

"Where is he?"

"He's gone. He left this letter for you." She pulled out a piece of paper and tucked it into CJ's hand. He started to muster the strength to move, fearing the pain it might bring. She pulled it back out. "Silly me. Maybe I should just read it to you."

He nodded.

"CJ, sorry you got shot, man. We can't stick around. Farseer says her destiny path leads her out of this city, whatever that means. She said your road goes a different direction now, but I couldn't leave without getting you to the hospital first. If you can move when you wake up, get out as soon as you can before they figure it out. If not, they'll probably take you back to jail, but, well, at least you'll be alive. When next we meet, maybe I'll be a Super. Isn't that crazy? Thanks for all your advice, George Imhoff."

Delia had a tear in her eye. "Why'd you have to leave the jail? Your lawyer was working on an appeal. Now…"

"Now, I have to get out of here." As he listened to the letter, CJ seemed to wake up for the second time. His dire circumstances started to override his pain.

"No way. You just had surgery on your chest. The bullet punctured one of your lungs. If you tear the wound open, you'll drown in your own blood."

CJ thought she never looked more beautiful. "If I go back, it'll be for twenty years at least. I'll never see you again. I wouldn't even *let* you wait for me that long."

Delia used a tissue to wipe away her tear. "It doesn't matter. You can't move. You have nowhere to go. They'd find you at your apartment or mine. They'll find you anywhere. You might as well turn yourself in. Can't you say that old woman mind-controlled you or something? If you turn yourself in, they might believe that."

CJ shook his head. "It doesn't matter, I'm just too tired. I couldn't move if I wanted to. Don't leave me. Please. Stay until…"

"I won't leave." She laid her warm cheek against his, gently touching his ear with her nose.

He clung to that moment of bliss as the drugs carried him away again.

WHEN HE NEXT WOKE, DAYLIGHT STREAMED IN THROUGH THE WHITE CURTAINS. He turned to see Delia and instead saw Juliet.

"Hi, Daddy! You're up." She put her phone away and stood next to him. "I'm glad you're alive."

"Thanks. Me, too. It's great to see you." After a moment, he asked, "Where's…"

"She's eating. I came by to give her a break."

"Cool. Aren't you supposed to be in school?"

She shook her head. "I think this is just a little bit more important, don't you?"

He nodded. Even that hurt. "I love you. Thanks so much for coming."

"Well, I don't know if I'll get many more chances to see you." Juliet had a flat smile. It spoke volumes about her disappointment. She knew he was supposed to be in jail and next time it would be for a lot longer.

"I'm sorry about that. I didn't mean… I really thought this job with Farseer was going to work out. People were coming to her for powers. I thought for sure they'd all see her as a hero and…"

"I know. I thought it would be the job you've been looking for your whole life, too." Juliet took his hand in her cold fingers. "It'll be okay, Dad."

"I don't think it will. I think…"

"It will." She lifted her chin as she said it. That was how his ex said things when she wasn't going to argue any more. "Right now, just rest."

"I'm hungry, and still tired even though I slept for like a day."

She held the water up to his lips. It had ice in it now and didn't taste stale.

"Thanks. So much. I wish I could be the father you deserve."

"You have been." He knew she just said that because he was recovering from a bullet wound, but he let it warm his heart a little anyway. "So what was all this business about people glowing?"

"That's part of Farseer's process. There are three gates and each time you pass one you glow red for a few seconds. I guess I passed the second gate. I figured out Rack's weakness and how to escape."

"How?"

"It's my power, I guess. It's all kind of confusing. But it doesn't matter now, since Farseer's gone I won't get to finish."

"She has to be there for it to work?"

"I think so. She always was."

"And you know Rack's weakness now?"

"For all the good it will do me."

Her pocket vibrated. She held up a finger and pulled out the phone, typing a few short words before replacing it.

"You're not like a kid at all," he said. "You're like an adult in a twelve-year-old body."

She gave him a crooked smile, then rolled her eyes like any pre-teen would do when their parents say something ridiculous. "I'm just glad you're going to get better."

She held his hand as he drifted back to sleep.

HE WOKE A FEW HOURS LATER, IN THE AFTERNOON, JUDGING BY THE PROGRAM Delia was watching on TV. "I can't believe those court shows are legal."

She switched it off. "It's interesting to watch how people's lives fall apart and what they do to put them back together again."

"Well, the falling apart I got down. The putting back together, not so much."

She put one hand on his head, smoothing his wild hair. "Let's just be grateful you're alive. The surgeon said if that had been a newer taxi, made of lighter material, the bullet probably would have gone all the way to your heart and you'd be dead."

"Lucky shot." CJ shrugged, then wished he hadn't. "How long am I supposed to be in here?"

"Well, assuming they don't figure out your real name isn't Anthony Clarkston, they said you'd be in here for at least two weeks. Although, they are planning to move you to a regular room in another day or so."

"How long before they realize I'm not Anthony Clarkston?"

"As soon as the cops figure out only one of the jailbirds is with Farseer and come looking for the second one, probably. Rack knows he shot the taxi, so they shouldn't have much trouble tracking down the driver, which would lead them here. Alternatively, the real Anthony Clarkston will probably report all his cards stolen. When he finds out somebody is using his insurance, they'll come here looking for you. Either way, they'll tack identity theft and insurance fraud on to your growing list of felonies."

CJ took a deep breath, then exhaled when his chest burned. "I've got no choice. I have to turn myself in."

"That's the smart thing to do."

"I can't believe Farseer just up and left me."

"She didn't have a choice either. They have been looking for her non-stop for 24 hours. When the governor found out what she was doing, making more Supers, she sent every cop in the state after her."

"They'll never find her. But, why are they after her?"

"They don't want her making more Supers."

"Why not?"

"I guess they are afraid of what all the new Supers might do."

"Same thing the current Supers do. Except with more of them, the few we have now wouldn't be so special."

"You really believe in her?"

"I believe she's doing the right thing. I hope they don't catch her."

Delia pushed his hair back with her hand and kissed his forehead. "It's nice to see you believing in something."

"I believe in God."

She smiled. "Farseer didn't leave you empty handed." She pulled another small leather pouch out of her purse and held it up.

"More gems? How many."

"An even dozen. All different colors."

CJ smiled. "She's the best boss I ever had. She's more of a hero than any of these spandex wrapped glory hogs."

"I haven't had them appraised yet. But it's probably about twenty-four thousand, if they're worth what the first three were."

CJ did the math in his head. "So you keep one for you and one for me when I get out… if I ever get out. Give the rest to Lexi. That should get Juliet most of the way through high school. On second thought, give her every-thing but yours. You can sell yours, too, of course, if you want."

"I don't need one."

"I want you to have one to remember me by. You'll have to find a new guy, somebody with a good job who wants to stay home and raise kids and read the newspaper every morning."

"Nobody reads the newspaper anymore."

"Whatever. You know what I mean." CJ took her hand. He felt his own heart breaking. "I want you to be happy. I know I can't be there for you now, but you must keep one of those gems. That way, there will be one thing you can look at sometimes and remember me and that in the end I did something right by you."

"We don't need to figure all of that out now," she said. "For now, I'm just grateful you're alive."

"Promise me you'll keep one. It's important to me."

"Okay. Thank you." She leaned over and kissed him.

The door opened and they both looked up. CJ expected to see a nurse. Instead, he saw a gorgeous blonde woman in a high fashion red dress and high heels.

"I'm not interrupting anything, am I?"

They both stared. Delia stood.

CJ said, "Do I know you?"

"Probably."

He looked more closely at her diamond and ruby encrusted necklace. It

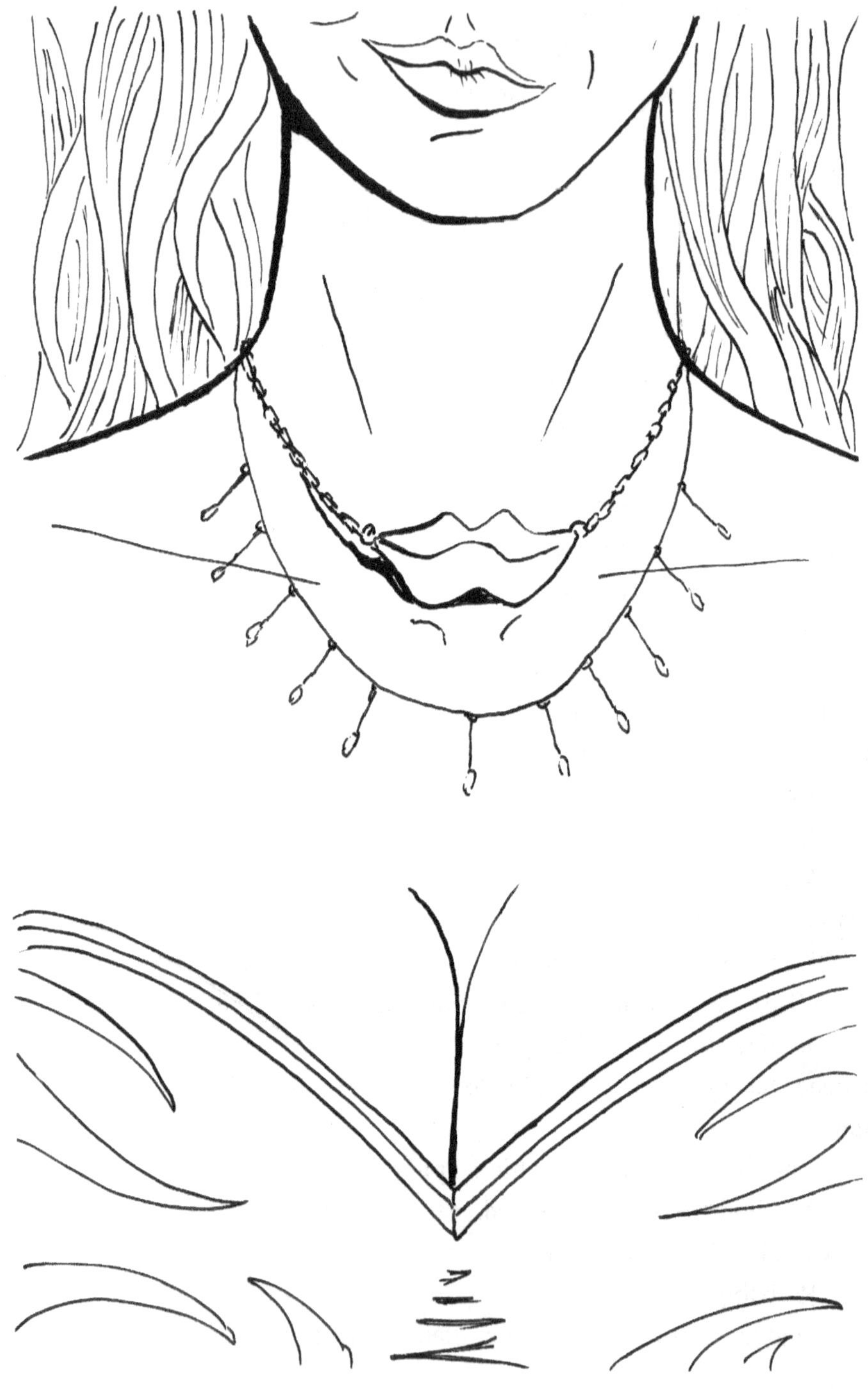

featured voluptuous lips and the letters KS. It was a logo he'd seen before. He snapped his fingers. "Katie Siren, high fashion Super."

She beamed a movie star smile and flipped a lock of hair behind one ear. "A little birdy told me you need a job."

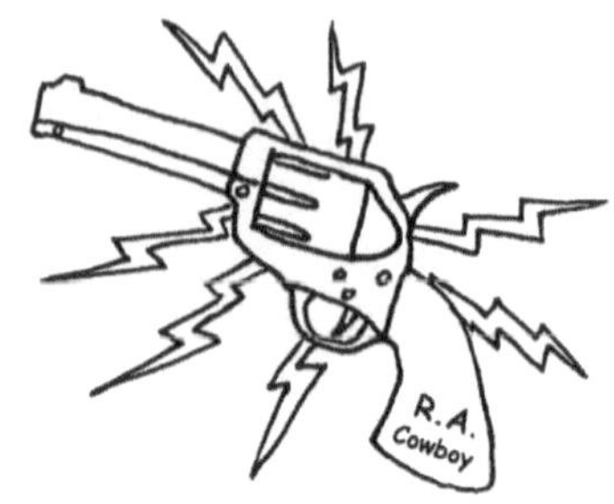

15

"**Y**ou can't be serious," Delia said. "Look at him. He's in no condition to do anything."

Katie Siren gazed down her pert nose and let the smallest hint of a smile crack her fire engine red lips. "I am."

"What could you possibly need me for?" CJ had to work hard to remember details through the drug-induced stupor. "You have tons of people working for you."

"True." She looked at her fingernails as if this was already boring her.

"What could you possibly want from me?"

"I have it on good authority that you know how to defeat Rack."

CJ's eyes went wide. Delia looked at him with a scowl. "It's true. I do. But how did you find out?"

"I told you, a little bird told me."

"A little bird?"

"Well, not a real bird. Somebody called Stormcrow gave me the tip."

"Stormcrow?" CJ felt like his mind was rusty gears and he had to push really hard to make them turn. George? It made sense. He was working for Farseer, and he was already planning to become a Super, based on what he said in the letter Delia read. Obviously, he took a name that matched Farseer, and vaguely matched his Hispanic origin. Was he planning to be her sidekick? Had he already passed the second gate? The third? CJ came back to his own thoughts. "So if I tell you how to beat Rack, you'll get me out of here and give me a job when you take over Denver?"

"Obviously."

Delia frowned. "How can you get him out of here?"

Katie rolled her eyes. "You let me take care of the little details, honey. What do you say?"

CJ looked at Katie and then Delia. He didn't want to work for Katie Siren. He wanted to keep working for Farseer, but that ship had sailed. He knew Katie had the resources to help him escape. What did it matter now if he was caught trying to leave the hospital? Compared to the charges he already faced, this was nothing.

Delia leaned down and whispered, "The judge won't be lenient this time. If you get arrested working with another Supervillain…"

"I know," CJ said. He gave her a short kiss on the cheek. Guilt washed through him, but he forced it back. "But what difference does it make now? This way, I might have a chance with you."

She began to cry. "This is no chance."

CJ turned to Katie. "I accept. But you have to get me out of here before I tell you."

"Of course. It's not like I can't put you right back if you lie." She smiled again, and walked out.

CJ heard her talking to somebody in the hall. Then three men, two in blue scrubs and one in a white doctor's coat came in. The doctor said, "It's time to move to your new room."

CJ squeezed Delia's hand as she backed up. The doctor removed the tube from CJ's chest, which hurt a lot and felt weird, before patching it up. The men in scrubs released wheels on the bottom of his bed and turned him toward the wide door. The doctor unplugged the monitors and grabbed the I.V. stand, wheeling it behind them so they didn't have to pull the needle out of CJ's arm.

Katie was already gone. They all paused by the nurse's station. The doctor signed two papers. Then he took a manila file folder and tossed it on the bed next to CJ's feet. "We'll keep in touch."

Then the bed lurched. CJ felt that one in his chest. The two men wheeled him out two sets of double doors, past a loading zone in an underground parking lot, and into a waiting ambulance. Delia appeared out the back

doors. She was crying and smiling at the same time. He wanted to hug her and tell her it would be okay. She looked ready to break into hysterics. He waved feebly. "I'll call you."

She bit her lip. "I love—"

The doors closed. The vehicle leaped forward, and soon they were out into the daylight, driving away from the hospital.

LESS THAN AN HOUR LATER, CJ WAS IN A NEW BED IN A ROOM WITHOUT WINDOWS. He didn't know where. A box of I.V. solution sat next to a new I.V. stand that didn't have wheels. His file lay on the carpet next to it.

He had a television he didn't feel like watching. He knew he should probably sleep, but he couldn't stop running through the events of the day. How had George even known Katie Siren to contact her? How had George thought of such a plan? Maybe his new power helped. Either way, he was a good friend and CJ owed him.

The door swung open, grabbing CJ's attention.

Katie stepped through wearing the same killer red dress. "This room is really ugly." She turned back to somebody CJ couldn't see. "Get some pictures in here. Oh, and diffuse lighting."

"Thanks for all of this," CJ said. "Without you..."

"You'd be spending the rest of your life in prison." She stopped smiling. "I know. That's the kind of loyalty only money can buy."

CJ tried to smooth his hair. He felt uncouth in every way. "So, Rack's weakness?"

She smiled again. "Yes?"

"His real powers are luck and evasion. The random thing is just something he's learned to do because it gives his powers more chances to work. If there's any way for an attack against him to go wrong, it will. If there's any chance of his own to work, it will. Without his powers, he's probably a terrible shot. But by luck, he hits every time."

Katie's tongue touched the side of her mouth as she thought about what he said. "That's useful, but not really a weakness."

"I know. But you have to understand that for the weakness to make sense. The only way to beat him is with a distraction. He relies too much on his erratic behavior to channel his powers. So if you get him focused on something else, you can create an opening."

"That's how you managed your great escape?" She looked at his bandaged chest and tipped her head. "I'm sure I can manage a distraction or ten, but it's not really my style. You sure there's not something more concrete?"

CJ shook his head. "The only other way would be a fail-proof plan. If there literally is no possible way for him to evade or escape, then his powers wouldn't save him. But that's a logistical conundrum."

Katie slowly wagged her head back and forth. "Silly little man. Fool-proof plans are my specialty." She favored him with a dazzling smile that showed perfect teeth.

"Of course." CJ thought she was barking up the wrong tree if she tried to concoct some perfect trap, but she was the boss. He was in no position to question her.

"Now, there's another little matter we need to discuss," she said. She looked at the chair against the wall, as if considering if she wanted to sit down for this part. She obviously found it distasteful and turned her attention back to him. "I need you to tell me my weakness."

"What?"

"Well, it's obvious this is your power."

CJ scrunched up his forehead. "You think every Super has a weakness?"

"It stands to reason," Katie said.

"Why wouldn't we have heard of it before?" CJ quickly thought of all the information he'd collected on Supers over the years. Did they all have hidden weaknesses? If they did, it was the best cover-up in history.

"I don't think it's something Supers want widely published. Besides, most of them probably don't know their own weakness. They naïvely think they are infallible."

"And you think my power will tell what could defeat all of them?"

"Assuming they all have one, yes. I'm not stupid enough to think I'm any exception. So read me. How would you defeat me?"

"Actually, I can't tell your weakness."

"Why? I will consider it an act of disloyalty if you refuse to help me. I don't really want a sidekick, of course, but a power like yours could be worthy of a position in the company. Junior partner?"

"Believe me, if I could, I would tell you, but I don't have my power. It worked once on Rack because of the second gate."

"The what?" Her eyes held contempt and contemplation in equal amounts. He really wanted to swing that pendulum to the contemplation side.

"That's what Farseer called them. The red glowing. It has to happen three times to get your power. It only happened twice for me. So I learned what my power *would be* when I saw Rack's weakness, but I can't do it again until I pass the third gate. And since Farseer's gone now, I probably can't."

Katie stared into his eyes. He could see her mind running through dozens of plans and ideas. It was awe inspiring and fearsome. He never wanted to be on her bad side. "So you have to see Farseer again to finish cooking? I've got people combing this city to find and watch every one of the people Farseer did her magic on. But in a city full of Supers, I need to know my own weakness, so I can protect myself from the hordes of would-be usurpers."

"That would help," he said. The tiny crow's feet by her eyes smoothed out again. CJ didn't want her messing with Farseer's hopefuls, but he wasn't in a position to say so.

"We will have to arrange your reunion with her later. It will take time for all the new Supers to figure out what's going on. If they are in the same boat as you, most of them won't have their powers yet, right?"

"I assume so. But one guy for sure got them already. Travis Mueller."

"We knew about him. He punched Rack off the horse. I've got people looking for him now. I'm going to hire him, if he's sensible."

"Anything I can do in the meantime?"

Katie put her long fingers on her chin as if thinking, but CJ suspected she already worked all this out in her master plan. "You just need to get better. I can get Super strong people anywhere, but if you really can tell me every Super's weakness, your power is a rare gift. Once I get things sorted out here and you're up and moving around, we'll arrange another meeting with Farseer."

"Okay." CJ glanced at the blank television. He would be watching a lot of it for the next couple of weeks, it seemed. That would give him time to take in everything that had happened.

"In the meantime, I have an assistant here for you. Her name is Maude."

Katie put one hand out and a middle-aged woman in a white shirt and pink skirt came in. She had a caring smile. In her hands, she held the television remote and a mug. "She'll take care of anything you need. I'll let you know if I want anything else in the meantime."

Katie yanked the door closed on her way out.

"I thought you might start with some broth," Maude said. She had a high voice, which CJ suspected was cultivated to sound kind no matter what she said or felt. "The sooner we get you back on solid foods, the sooner you can take out that I.V. catheter."

"Okay," CJ said. "Can we turn on the news, too? I think I have a lot to catch up on."

She clicked several buttons and adjusted the volume. Then she put a straw into the mug and held it to his lips. It tasted like heaven.

The reporter said, "Random Acts of Cowboy has been patrolling the streets off and on. Although police have said they have several leads on the missing Supervillain, they are certain she has left the state."

"It's certainly hard to believe all that," Maude said. "My friend said she heard the woman was turning people into Supers. Not sure, but that doesn't sound like the act of a villain. What do you think?"

CJ took a deep breath. It still hurt, but he was adjusting to the pain. "I think the whole problem all along has been people trying to insist that all Supers are either a hero or a villain."

"How's that?"

CJ suspected Maude was drawing him out on purpose to get him talking, but he couldn't resist. He launched into his lecture about why Supers shouldn't be called heroes or villains.

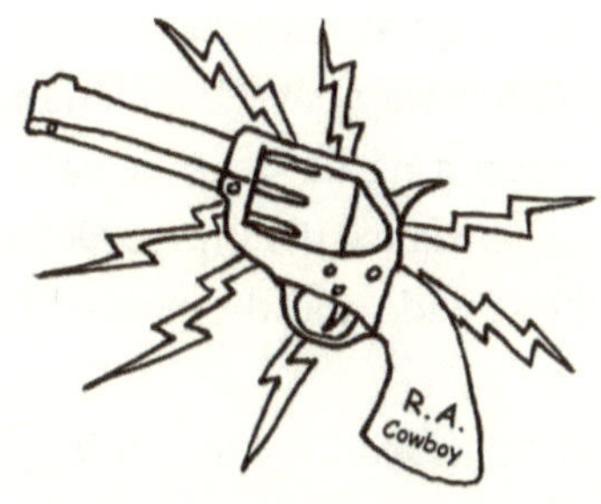

16

he problem with so-called heroes is that they can only react. The so-called villain gets to make the plans. How much of a hero can you be if you never have any plans?" Maude's wandering eyes told CJ she was no longer listening. "I just need to go out and walk around. I'm going crazy in this little room." It had been almost a week and CJ was starting to wish he'd gone to prison instead.

"I'm sorry, but Ms. Siren said she doesn't want you leaving this room until she comes back."

"Why? What's the point in that?"

"She's got a lot on her plate right now, and I think she wants to be with you when you see the rest of the building."

"What's out there?" CJ demanded. Maude had been great, but he was getting tired of her babying him. What was Katie hiding? He knew part of the answer: she was hiding a lot. He just didn't know why she felt the need to hide it from him. Obviously, she wasn't going to trust him until he was a full Super. How much would she really trust him if he knew her weakness?

"Nothing important, but you know her. She's very specific about people following her directions. She'll come for you when she's ready. Until then..."

"Make do. Yeah, I know." CJ sat up and dangled his feet over the side of the bed. "Can you at least get a card table and some cards or something? If I have to watch daytime television for one more day, I'm liable to hurt myself."

Maude smiled. "Sure. I'll go see what I can do."

She locked the door on her way out. CJ rolled his eyes and plopped back on the bed, immediately regretting the pain he caused himself. He coughed once, suppressing any more because the image Delia put into his mind about tearing the surgical stitches inside and drowning on his own blood terrified him.

When she returned, Maude had a card table. She didn't set it up, just leaned it against the wall beneath a picture of the ocean flanked by palm trees. "Good news. Ms. Siren is on her way down."

When she came in, CJ expected Katie to be wearing red again. This time she wore an iridescent cobalt blue dress with matching heels. "How are you feeling?"

"Better." CJ took a deep breath, as if the ability to do so would prove something.

"Good. I want your help."

Maude said, "He's not really well enough to move yet."

Katie looked at her as she spoke, then snapped her head toward CJ. "Is this true?"

"I can do some things."

"He can sit. He shouldn't walk far. He can't bend or lift anything. It will be another two weeks at least before he's able to be up and around. It will be a few months before he's back to full strength." Maude wasn't trying to protect him. She was just doing her job.

"Can he at least sit in a chair somewhere else?" Katie looked at her metallic blue nail polish. CJ thought it made her look cyanotic.

"He should be okay with that for a little while."

"Good. Bring him to the command office in the next five minutes."

CJ smiled. He knew he shouldn't push it, but he wanted to see anything besides this small room. He put his feet over the side of the bed.

"Whoa." Katie held up a hand. "You need to get dressed. I have a reputation to uphold." As she left, she said, "Maude, come with me."

Maude followed her out and returned with a pinstriped suit in a clear suit bag on hangers. She had a duffle bag in the other hand. "We better hurry if you're going to be ready in five minutes."

CJ smiled. He always liked working for people who wanted him to look nice.

By the time Maude had him dressed, CJ was exhausted and hurting. She gave him a handful of pills, which he downed with a bottle of water. She fussed with his hair, putting in some gel and then making it even messier.

"Shouldn't I shave?" CJ looked at himself in the mirror. He'd never had somebody use product to make his hair stick up on one side.

"This is Katie Siren," Maude said. "Think extreme fashion."

"So goofy hair and short beard?"

"Yes. And that suit was probably a thousand dollars."

"Wow." CJ looked at it again, coifing the pink thing sticking out of the front pocket. It matched the tie. "She outfits all her crew with clothes this expensive?"

"They all dress nice, but you're special, so it has to be extra high quality."

She meant it as a compliment, but concern crept in when he heard it. He made his living by being one of the nameless underlings. Being in the spotlight drew all kinds of unwanted attention. "Well, let's get going."

He stood up and tested his feet in the shiny black shoes. They felt surprisingly good. Maude insisted on walking right beside him, holding one arm. Once they left the room, CJ was disappointed to find a hall that went to an elevator. After so long, he expected something fantastic like a warehouse full of weapons.

He tried to look strong, but by the time they reached the elevator, he had to lean heavily on the rail to rest. Maude had to put in a special key in order to push the second highest button. When the doors opened, CJ finally surrendered and said, "Can I wait for just a minute."

"Of course." Maude held the door as it tried to close several times. When CJ went through, he felt like he'd walked into a NASA control center. How had she set all this up so quickly?

Banks of computers ran along the inside of the room, leaving the outside open. They were in a high rise, with a stunning view of the city. The day was overcast, but clear. CJ could see for miles to the northwest. They were in the business district in one of the highest buildings, which meant she'd managed to get her hands on some very expensive real estate in the Spire and convert it from a condo to a command office on very short notice.

"I'm used to being higher up," Katie said, "but this was the best the city could offer. You will sit here." She indicated a plush executive chair surrounded by monitors mounted on a tall frame.

CJ smiled, and tried not to let his relief show as he sat on the chair and let it lean back. He could sleep right then if they'd let him. "This is great."

"The main computer screen shows a small view of all the others. You can just touch any one of them and it will show up on the big central screen." She reached a perfectly manicured hand out and demonstrated. The image of a man on a motorcycle, sitting in traffic, filled the large central screen above.

CJ leaned back and interlocked his fingers. "Excellent."

Katie ignored him. She held up a headset. "Put this on. If you see anything in all these videos that I need to know about, push this red button. It will patch you in to me directly. You are on an over-ride, which means anybody else I'm talking to will be muted. I don't think I have to tell you how important it better be before you push this button. Whatever you have to say after, say it quick, then let go of the button. I'll contact you if I want more information after that." She set the device in his hands and fussed with his hair a little bit. "Maude, you did well considering the time crunch, but we really must get him to a proper stylist soon. Those fingernails are ghastly."

"I'll put it on the schedule," Maude said with a smile. CJ didn't know what Katie was paying her, but it probably wasn't enough.

Katie walked over to a larger bank of monitors holding a custom remote. She put on her own headset. It was sleek to the point of being almost invisible. Track lighting hit her iridescent dress from every angle, making her sparkle like she was on stage. She pointed the remote at one of the monitors. CJ's face, in profile, filled her center screen. When he turned back toward the camera, Katie's face filled his own large monitor. "CJ, if you would do the honors, select screen three and push the green button."

CJ touched the small picture, labeled 3. It brought up a construction site. The lower portion of a new building with steel girders sticking out above concrete walls came up large. A crane on one side and a cement truck on the other framed the project. *Thou shalt not kill.* He didn't see any people. On the touch screen, a green circle appeared. CJ felt his stomach go sour and he shook his head a little. He reached out a finger and touched the green button.

The walls exploded, engulfing the skeleton of the unfinished building in bright fire. It peeled the paint on the nearby crane and overturned the cement truck. The camera zoomed out, showed a huge mushroom of black smoke rising.

Katie's face appeared again for a few seconds. "Nice work, CJ. Okay, everybody, the game is on."

The monitors all came alive with activity. Two screens showed motorcycle riders, one in red, the other in green, weaving through slow traffic. Large tractors on another screen growled to life. Snipers gave the thumbs up. Small strike teams on top of buildings or secreted in alleyways saluted. Katie's plan was vast and, for better or worse, in motion.

CJ was thrilled at the symbolic expression of power. He'd never set off a huge explosion like that before. He knew why she'd afforded him this special honor. Now he was complicit in her plan, whatever it might be. He tried to add up the number of years he would get if they arrested him now, then stopped. He'd be in jail for life. The next time he saw a prison, it would be the last thing he ever saw.

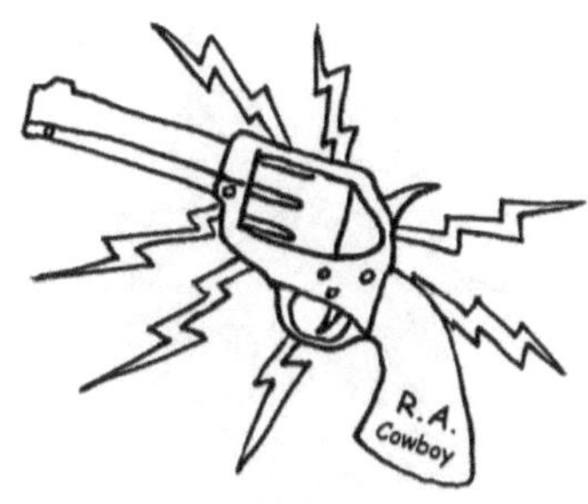

17

CJ looked from screen to screen, trying to piece together the puzzle of Katie's plan. Both motorcyclists rode past the bombsite, then headed away in different directions. They were meant to look like they were responsible.

As one rode away on the main roads, the other weaved in and out of smaller back streets. The camera angles changed often. Apparently, Katie's people had hacked into numerous security feeds around the city, giving them a decent picture of everything as it happened.

For a minute, it looked as if nobody even noticed. Then a lone police car pulled up to the now smoldering fire. Before the fire trucks arrived, a man on a nearby roof came into the picture. He had a cowboy hat in his hands, and though too small to identify positively by the camera image, Katie's voice came through the speakers: "There's the target."

Rack used his high vantage point to scan the city, identifying the red motorcyclist who was zig-zagging through a housing district. He left the tall building in a rush.

A few minutes later, two men mounted on horses arrived on the main road at the edge of the neighborhood. When the motorcyclist emerged, he was caught between two Old West lawmen. The camera angle here was wide, giving the whole picture, but few details. The motorcyclist gunned his engine, then left a small cloud of smoke as he bolted forward, as if planning to jump off the side of the road. He turned at the last second, heading along the road at high speed, planning to go around the outside of Rack.

Rack shot out the front tire. In a big tumbling mess, the red motorcycle flipped, sending the rider sliding along the pavement as pieces of the bike skidded along the road and off the edge of the raised street.

Before anybody reacted, the green motorcycle streaked by going at least ninety miles per hour. Rack ran after the green rider, waving for Deputy Knight to tend to the red one.

Slowing at the next crossroad, the green rider disappeared between two tall buildings, riding the center yellow lines to avoid cars going both directions.

One of the previously unmoving camera feeds followed Rack as his horse jumped off the side of the street and cut down the berm and across a few yards filling the wedge shape between the crash site and the green rider's new path.

Among houses, the number of cameras available diminished, sometimes leaving the view empty. Katie's techs always managed to get ahead of the action before long, though.

Rack jumped onto the far street a few seconds too late to intercept the green cycle. The two screens merged, then the motorcycle bobbed to the side and rode up a tight alley between two buildings.

Rack followed, scoping out the path. He wasted two seconds, trotting his horse in a circle, before turning to the side and galloping off in a different direction.

He's using his power. Knowing a horse was never fast enough to catch a motorcycle, Rack had chosen a seemingly random course. Yet, a few seconds later, the camera showed he'd gone exactly the right direction to intercept the approaching bike.

"Head for the end site," Katie said. The motorcycle changed tactics. Instead of turning onto the street where Rack waited in ambush, the bike leapt up and crossed the road into a parking lot. Blasting between cars, it slalomed through the lot, avoiding people and concrete barriers.

Rack raised his pistol, obviously annoyed, and spurred his horse to charge after the man in green, leaping onto grass and crossing expanses the motorcycle had to go around. The chase led them through the middle of the University of Colorado campus. The motorcycle forced students off the sidewalk as it revved between orange brick buildings and green trees.

The Spire appeared in the background of the low angle camera following Rack. They weren't far from him. Rack stayed on the grass between two walkways gaining distance on the motorcycle, which had to deal with people.

The rider turned between two buildings.

Rack turned one building sooner, putting himself in the way to stop the motorbike from doubling back.

The motorcycle came out in a construction zone where the university was putting up a new building. The sleek vehicle zipped between two over-sized bulldozers with six-foot high shovel blades.

Seeing no way around, Rack headed for the same opening. At the last second, one of the tractors lurched forward, closing the gap. Rack's horse turned to the side, only to find two more earthmovers rolling into place. All the drivers jumped out and ran.

Only when Rack was completely surrounded by a square of tall, concave metal walls, did CJ grasp the full extent of Katie's plan. There were small cat's eye shaped openings Rack might escape between, if he left his horse behind. Or he could try and climb over the huge blades, but Katie had all of those openings covered by snipers.

"If he tries to escape, take the shot," she ordered.

CJ pushed the green button. "Tell them to stay behind cover." Katie turned to him; her brows knit.

Several shots echoed through the microphone feed. Rack's guns waved over the top of the machines. One sniper took a hit to the arm and fell back.

"Stay down!" Katie repeated into her headset. She pointed at one of the sniper cameras and it grew large in her center screen. The sniper had one hand over his arm, staunching the profuse flow of blood. She switched back to the view of Rack. "Keep him covered, but don't expose yourself."

Two more shots from Rack ricocheted off concrete walls.

CJ was glad he could help in some small way. His head was swimming. He had a constant pain in his chest that reminded him he really hoped Katie took Rack out. The cowboy dismounted, creeping toward one of the openings.

CJ hit the button again. "He'll get out through the opening not being covered."

Katie pulled up a previously stagnant screen. "Alpha team, cover the southwest corner."

The tall machines blocked their view as a firefight started up. Rack managed to hit three men before their heavy onslaught brought him down. When the smoke cleared, the last two members of the attack team, dressed in black, moved forward with their automatic weapons trained on Rack.

The woman in the lead tapped her ear and said into the microphone. "He's down, bleeding from a head wound. You want us to finish him?"

Katie paused, tapping her lips. "No. Patch him up and bring him to me. If we're going to make a go of things in this city, people have to stop seeing me as a villain."

"Roger."

WHEN CJ FINALLY RETURNED TO HIS ROOM, HE FOUND ANOTHER BED. MAUDE WAS leaning over it, fussing with her watch as she held up the other patient's wrist to check a pulse. One glance confirmed CJ now shared a room with Rack. Lucky for the cowboy, CJ wasn't the vengeful type.

So tired he didn't really care, CJ let himself down onto the bed still wearing the thousand-dollar suit. Knowing Rack's powers, he had to ask one question. "He has a head wound?"

Maude turned with her permanent smile. "Yes. Just glanced him, but it was enough head trauma to put him in a coma. He's very lucky. If the bullet had been a little bit in any other direction, he'd have died. All the other bullets missed major organs and arteries, too."

"He's lucky like that," CJ said. Then he closed his eyes and trusted Katie had the sense to restrain Rack. He was too tired to check.

WHEN HE WOKE, CJ FOUND MAUDE HAD REMOVED HIS SUIT WITHOUT WAKING HIM. Rack was still unconscious in the bed next to him. CJ lay still for a while, looking at the long hair poking out from the white bandage on Rack's head. They hadn't hooked up an I.V. or any other equipment.

CJ was glad to find he was wearing blue sweats now, instead of a hospital gown. He slowly sat up and then stood. He didn't feel good, by any stretch of the imagination, but he could get to the bathroom without calling for Maude.

When he came out, Katie and Maude were there. Katie had on a black dress and prominent silver jewelry. Her heels weren't as high as usual.

"There you are," Katie said. "We're moving your roommate out. Hope you don't mind."

CJ smiled at her sarcasm. "Where to?"

"Actually, I'm having him taken to St. Luke's Hospital. There's a whole media circus. You can watch it." A silver bracelet dangled from her wrist as she pointed to the television.

A few men in suits came in. They released the brakes and rolled Rack's bed out. CJ turned on the television. He opened a warm bottle of water from the counter and sat back down on the bed. He was starving but he wouldn't bother Maude with that until she got back.

"We're live in front of the Spire in the business district, where visiting fashion mogul, Katie Siren, has called for a press conference. There is an ambulance waiting nearby. At this time, we have no idea why it's in this area." The reporter put her hand over the earpiece and looked to the side for a moment. "I'm told she's coming out now."

The camera moved to the front door of the condominiums where a few men opened the door and Katie walked out. She had her movie star smile on and gave a small wave to the news camera. Behind her, they rolled out the bed with Rack lying on it. Between CJ's room and the door, somebody had put his cowboy hat over his stomach and propped his hands to hold it down.

Katie stepped up to a podium set up on the concrete entry with three microphones sticking out. "Good morning. I'm Katie Siren. I recently came to Denver to look into the possibility of expanding my corporation to this fine city. Before I even had a chance to meet with state officials, several of my people found this Superhero bleeding and unconscious not far from here. My personal physician patched him up. As soon as she determined he was safe to move, we arranged to have him transported to a local hospital." She put out one hand to indicate the bed rolling toward a waiting ambulance.

The camera zoomed in on Rack's face, the moustache taking prominence in the shot as the bed rolled toward the open back doors. They filmed the paramedics collapsing the bed and rolling it inside the vehicle.

"I don't know who shot Random Acts of Cowboy." The camera swiveled back to Katie's perfect face and hair. "I only know if my security people hadn't found him when they did, he probably would have died. I'm just grateful we were in the right place at the right time to keep such a great hero alive. But I've been mobilizing my people to help keep Denver safe from villains now that Rack is clearly unable to do the job."

Several reporters raised their hands to ask questions. Katie pointed to one.

"Considering you've been labeled a Supervillain for things that happened in New York last year, what proof can you give us that you aren't responsible for what happened to Rack?"

18

"The allegations of my supposed Supervillainy in New York have been definitively proven false according to the court ruling in which I successfully sued those slanderers." Katie's smile never wavered. "Are there any questions about the events at hand?"

Another reporter asked, "Why didn't you call an ambulance yesterday when you found him?"

"As I stated, I have a personal physician. Her professional medical opinion, for which we are happy to provide certification, was that he was in too delicate a position to move. Because of a head trauma, she felt it would be better to wait for him to stabilize before moving."

"Where's Deputy Knight?" This reporter shouted before Katie finished.

"I don't know where he is now. Information I recently uncovered indicates Rack and Deputy Knight were in pursuit of a pair of vandals. After catching the first one, they split up and Rack went after the second one alone. We can only assume the second one is responsible for Rack's current condition, although we have no evidence to prove it."

Several reporters raised their hands, but Katie didn't call on them. "I'm afraid I don't have much more information than what I've shared already."

"What are your plans for expanding Siren Cosmetics to Denver?" a young woman in the media crowd shouted.

Katie tipped her head toward the woman. "It's too early to make any official announcements, of course, but we are looking into opening a branch here. If we bring Siren Cosmetics to Denver, it will provide jobs for many residents and improve this city's standing in the fashion world. However, the feasibility of such a deal will depend on what kind of arrangements we can come to with the local politicians. Thank you for coming."

Katie waved and stepped down. The camera stayed on her until she went back in the Spire. Then it swooped to the ambulance and followed it out of the driveway and up the street. The reporter stepped back into the shot to repeat everything Katie said several times.

CJ BEGAN WORKING REGULARLY WITHIN A COUPLE WEEKS. FOR THE FIRST TIME IN his life, somebody else did the heavy lifting. All Katie expected him to do was help her monitor things. Once Rack was out of the way, she just ran her business like any other CEO.

She had agents scouting the city for buildings they could buy or lease. Her employees examined available factories and warehouses. Research looked into supply lines for distribution. Katie spent most of her time talking to other business owners and wealthy politicians at country clubs, fundraisers, and business meals. Sometimes she brought CJ along. He spent most of the time quietly absorbing the conversation, so he wouldn't make an idiot out of himself if somebody asked him a question. It only worked about half the time.

Every few days, Katie assigned CJ to a project. He had a new cell phone and contact list and a personal assistant, Jasmine, who knew everybody in the company and everything about their resources and processes. CJ's first paycheck was gigantic. He spent most of it on new suits, an expensive makeover, and a car. He felt guilty, but Jasmine made it clear Katie expected a certain standard.

"Here's the contact list for the county waste disposal company you requested," Jasmine said. She handed him a printed piece of paper. Despite being capable of using a computer, CJ still liked things he could touch whenever possible. He swiveled on his desk chair and accepted the page.

"Thanks. You could make these contacts better than me," CJ said. "Why didn't Katie just promote you and put me to work in the mail room?" He sat forward on the chair, trying not to crumple the suit jacket he'd perched there. He could handle the shiny red shirt and tie, but he only wore the coat to meetings or outside.

"If there's one thing I never doubt, it's Ms. Siren's decisions. She puts people exactly where she needs them."

"Why does she need me here?" CJ swiveled in his open office. He had most of the monitors off now, just using the one big one in the middle unless he had a reason. "I'm like a fish out of water."

"She must know you can fly with a little coaxing. Believe me, she's never wrong about things like this. In fact, she's never wrong about anything."

"I have an ex-wife like that." He swiveled back to his computer and picked up the phone. Jasmine went back to her desk set-up behind him, but within voice range.

Before he finished dialing, two of his monitors went on of their own accord. One showed a street corner from a security camera's view, the other had a close-up of Katie Siren wearing a peach silk dress that had frills over the shoulders. "Do you recognize this man?"

CJ studied the camera for a few seconds. The guy didn't have a full costume, just a cheesy t-shirt with black on one side and white on the other. His logo was a white M on the left side and a black square, set at an angle, with another M on the right. His face looked only vaguely familiar, but CJ couldn't put a name to it. "No. Sorry. He must be new. He's never been in Denver that I know of."

"He's started to become a thorn in my side." Katie tended to understate things like this, but CJ couldn't imagine how this guy could possibly upset so vast a corporation as hers. "Can you figure out how to dissuade him, by any chance?"

"I don't know, I can't tell from this video. You want me to go talk to him?" CJ knew he wasn't up to any kind of physical confrontation yet. His chest still hurt if he did anything strenuous, like putting on a shirt.

"Yes. Talk to him. Convince him to go be a Superhero somewhere else. If that doesn't work, figure out his Achilles' heel. If that doesn't work, go find Farseer so you can finally be of some use to me." Her call ended, but the video of the new MM continued to play.

CJ watched the man walk up to a pair of Katie's crew, surveying a building location from the street corner. They were just regular people, doing their jobs. The black-and-white shirted man walked up behind them and pulled a single pin from the tripod they used. The scope piece mounted on top tipped over the side. Before the two men could react and catch it, the lone Super grabbed a suitcase with their measurements and computer and jumped in his car.

The planned strike was fast and effective. Just like that, he'd brought this small piece of Katie's work to a dead stop. How many similar upsets had he caused? Obviously, his powers gave him a certain tactical advantage.

"Jasmine," CJ said, "I need a list of all the company's current little operations in this city. Also, get me a list of recent ones that this guy has upset."

"Okay," she called from her desk. "Give me a few minutes."

CJ watched the video again.

"Here you go," she said. He took two sheets of paper, still warm from the printer. One showed three current activities: an engineering appraisal for a factory in Globeville, a meeting between Katie and a delivery company executive, and CJ's planned visit to the water treatment facility. The "mysterious marauder", as CJ started calling him in his mind, wasn't likely to be at the executive meeting. CJ had a new assignment the guy couldn't know about, so he wouldn't be at the sewage plant. That left just the engineering appraisal.

Looking over the second paper, CJ couldn't help being impressed. Except for operations carried out in the Spire, or Katie's rich mingles, this mysterious marauder had managed to derail most of the company's efforts over the last few days. Assuming he was responsible for all of the setbacks, he'd upset hundreds of people's work.

"If she asks, tell her I'm in Globeville." CJ picked up his sport jacket and pulled it on slowly, taking care not to strain his healing lung.

Jasmine said, "I will. Is there anything you want me to do while you're gone?"

"Yes, actually. Can you call the sewer guy and set up a meeting for this afternoon? Try for lunch. If he won't do that, any time or anywhere, but no golf." CJ rubbed his chest.

"Okay. What time do you plan to be back?"

"I don't know. If I'm not back, you meet him. We just need some standard specs on how much and how fast for the current project considerations. I think five buildings. Katie wants them tomorrow, so buy an expensive lunch if he's willing."

"I will," Jasmine said. She looked proud, like he'd just promoted her. CJ smiled and headed for the elevator.

ALTHOUGH DENVER HAD PUT A LOT OF WORK INTO RENOVATING THE HISTORICAL areas, Globeville still had a large number of abandoned warehouses. For the first time in CJ's life, he felt out of place in a low-class part of town. He'd only been wearing designer suits for a week, and he just leased this fancy car two days ago. He knew what the locals would think when they saw him.

He noticed one warehouse just off the freeway had a lot of activity. It looked like pieces of airplane fuselage being delivered by flatbed truck. He exited the freeway at Dewey Lake and worked his way toward the property Siren Cosmetics was considering. He parked a block away, next to an active business. He pulled his jacket and tie off. Then he worked his way around behind one large building, so he could get a look at the place he was going. His leather shoes had terrible soles for sneaking and he suspected when one sunk into loose gravel that he might be ruining them. No time to change.

A group of women and men with hard hats went in through the front door. Moving closer, he looked up the street and saw the same blue car the mysterious marauder had used for the last hit.

Half-jogging, he went to the car. He found it unlocked with the suitcase/computer combo still on the back seat. Obviously planning for another quick escape, MM had left the keys in the car. CJ started it and drove it two blocks away, hiding it between two abandoned buildings. Then CJ took the keys. *Thou shalt not steal.* "It's not stealing if *he's* robbing *us*." He walked leisurely back toward the warehouse.

"Hey!" and "Stop! Thief!" echoed from inside the building. CJ saw the black and white t-shirt running out of the front door, carrying a tablet and a manila file folder.

CJ leaned against a lamppost, watching as the mysterious marauder stopped running halfway to his car. He put his arms out and spun around, as if unable to remember exactly where he put it. When the man finally accept-

M

ed the car was gone, his gaze focused on CJ.

CJ held up his new cell phone with a smile and put it to his ear. To the mysterious marauder he called out, "I can call the police now, unless you'd rather talk to me." CJ wouldn't call the police, of course, but this guy didn't know that.

"I can just run," the man said. He had a low voice, but it wavered insecurely.

"True. I'd never catch you in these shoes." CJ looked down. They were dusty, but he didn't think they were ruined yet. He held up the man's keys. "I have your car, though. I'm pretty sure the police can use it to track you down. I have video footage of you stealing from us. And those stolen goods are in the back of your car."

"What do you want?"

"I just want to talk. And I want that stuff you're carrying." The man threw the file and tablet down.

"See, that's making me think you'd rather talk to the cops. Why are you doing this? What do you have against Katie Siren?"

"She's a Supervillain. It's my duty to stop her."

"You think you're a Superhero? What's your name?"

"Mirror Max."

CJ didn't need his power to figure this guy out. The name was a dead giveaway. Apparently, he had the power to copy other Supers' powers. That would explain his nearly perfect tactical strikes against every one of Katie's operations even though his unshaven face and worn fingers looked more like a blue-collar man. He was copying her powers.

"What makes you think Katie's a villain? She's bringing new jobs and money to the city. How does that make her bad?"

"She doesn't care about the poor except as they serve her ends. Do you really think she'd keep you or anybody else around if they weren't making her rich and famous?"

If CJ hadn't been leaning against the post, he might have been pushed over by the force of Mirror Max's words. CJ had become the thing he'd always hated most.

19

CJ stared at Mirror Max, unsure what to do next. One of the women from inside the warehouse came out and picked up the file and tablet. She gave a nasty look to the would-be hero before marching indignantly back inside to finish her business.

CJ asked, "What makes you think you are the hero in this situation?"

"Because she is the bad guy," MM said.

"What has she done that's so bad?"

"She took out Rack. Nobody can prove it, but everybody knows it."

"And Rack was a hero so that makes her a villain and you a hero because you're against her?"

"Yes."

"Just like your logo and your shirt, you see everything as black and white. The M is white on both sides, though."

"Yes."

"How long have you been a Super?"

"About two weeks."

"Two weeks? So you're one of Farseer's people."

"Yes."

"How did you get past the gates?"

"Not that it's any of your business, but at my day job I'm a nurse. I happened to be on duty when Rack came in."

"You had passed two gates already?"

Mirror Max stared at the distant freeway. "No, only one. But when he showed up, I knew immediately that I could copy his powers and I glowed. I had the urge to do strange things, almost without knowing why. For no reason at all, I peeled up his bandages. One of the bullet wounds started to bleed. I glowed again."

"Blood of a Super. Wait, was Farseer around when this happened?"

"No."

CJ slapped his own forehead. How could he be so dumb? Why had he assumed she needed to be around? He began thinking through the situation. He could probably punch MM in the face right now and get his powers. Then he would know this guy's weakness. It was probably something ironic like he can't use his powers whenever he sees his reflection.

Although, MM's copying powers would mean after CJ became a Super, MM would know CJ's weakness, too, since he could copy CJ's power. Did MM have the same weakness as the Super he was mirroring? That would be important to know.

"Are you okay?" Mirror Max asked.

"Fine." CJ could discover Katie's weakness, but so could MM. CJ could tell Katie MM's weakness, too. But MM could probably tell Katie CJ's weakness. Did it even matter what their weaknesses were? They were all human-type Supers. A bullet could kill any one of them, regardless of their powers and weaknesses. CJ's head hurt. He liked working for Katie, but he didn't want her to be the ultimate Superpower in the world. If he told her every other Super's weakness, she would use that information to become the strongest. He could imagine less pretty overlords, but he didn't want anybody to be in that position, so he couldn't let himself become a Super as long as he worked for her.

MM tipped his head. "You don't seem fine."

"Rack shot me," CJ said. He unbuttoned his shirt and showed the huge bandage still on his chest. It wasn't bleeding anymore, but Maude insisted he keep a bandage with ointment on it to reduce the scarring. "He shot me in the chest because I was trying to get Farseer away from him before he killed her. Do you think Farseer was a villain?"

Mirror Max tipped his head up and took a deep breath. "No."

"Then Rack must be, right? That's how it works, according to what you said. And if Rack's a villain, that makes Katie a hero. So you trying to stop her, that makes you a villain."

MM scratched his chin. "Everybody knows Katie's a villain."

"How? Because some Supers said so? If you were a Supervillain, wouldn't your best move be to convince everybody that Superheroes were really the bad guys?"

"I… Maybe… I don't know."

"Think about it. You're copying her tactical genius right now, so tell me what you would do if you were a villain trying to bring her down?"

"Spread rumors?"

CJ snapped. "Exactly."

"But," Mirror Max held up one finger, "if I were a Supervillain and people exposed me, I'd say things like that to try and throw everybody off the trail."

CJ wanted to punch him in the face for two reasons now. "Don't be stupid! Are you a child? We can play who said what about whom all day and never come to any conclusion. Do you read the Bible? How does the Bible say we should judge people?"

"We shouldn't judge at all?"

"That, too. But by their fruits, right? Look at what they do to determine if they are good or bad. What did Farseer do?"

"She made me into a Super."

"Is that bad? Is she a villain?"

"No."

"Then if she's not a villain, why did Rack try and stop her?"

"I don't know."

"To keep the power for himself. All the Supers hate Farseer because they don't want us normals being like them. They want to be special. So they brand Farseer a villain and try to get us to condone them stopping her."

"So you're a normal?" MM said. "But we know Rack is a hero. He's brought down tons of villains, really bad ones."

"Sure," CJ said. He stood and stepped closer. "But if he was here now, and it was just you and Rack, what would he do to you? Would he help you or arrest you?"

"I don't know. Arrest me?"

CJ gave a thumbs up. "Katie has all the resources in the world. Right now, she's using them to help normal people in this city. Whatever else she's done, she's not a villain now. Personally, I don't think there even are heroes or villains. Just Supers and normals. You may have Katie's powers temporarily, but you don't have her resources. You can probably keep messing with her if you want. But if it comes to a battle, she's going to win. You'll be lucky if you end up in a coma with Rack. It will probably end worse."

Mirror Max looked at CJ and stepped closer. They were now only a few feet apart. "I don't have her powers anymore."

"What?" CJ furrowed his brow. "You just had them a few minutes ago. I saw you…"

"I know, but they are changing. I can feel it."

"Changing to what?"

"I don't understand it exactly." MM furrowed his brow. Then he pulled a box cutter out of his pocket. He flipped it open and sliced his finger.

"What are you doing?" CJ stepped back.

Max flipped blood onto CJ's face. CJ tasted coppery salt and felt his ears get hot while his mouth went dry.

CJ scrunched up his face. "Ew, gross! If you have some kind of a disease…"

"Blood from a Super. Welcome to the monkey house," MM said with a smirk. Red light glowed from CJ's hands, then spread all over his body.

CJ instantly knew two things. First, he knew that Mirror Max could copy his power or any Super's power he got close to, but he would always have the same weakness, not theirs. Second, he knew MM's weakness, and it came from the same power. Any time he was near normals that had begun but not finished the transformation into a Super, he would lose his power. With this information came a new insight into Supers CJ never suspected. Although Farseer was unlocking the power in normals to become Supers, many normals had the potential to become Supers on their own. For various reasons, they never realized their powers.

MM smiled. "Now we know each other better than we know ourselves. My boss will be happy to hear this."

"You know my weakness," CJ said. "But you won't forget it when you get close to another Super and change powers."

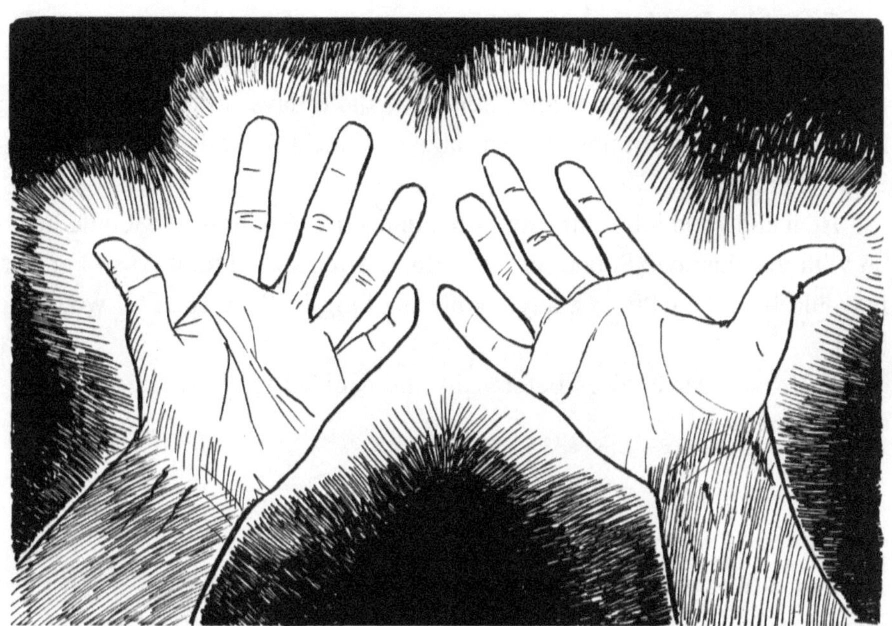

"Want to trade information?" Mirror Max looked manic now. Something about having CJ's power agitated him.

"You mean, tell each other our weaknesses?" CJ tried to focus his power inward and see what MM meant. Maybe he could detect his own. Nothing came to him.

"Sure. You go first."

MM laughed. "Actually, I already know mine. I figured it out while you were going on and on about labels."

"So what's mine?"

MM turned and ran.

CJ SAT IN HIS CAR A LONG TIME. HE WAS IN NO SHAPE TO RUN ANYBODY DOWN ON foot, so he let Mirror Max go. He went to a drive-through for lunch, and used the napkin to wipe Max's blood off his face. He drove to the top of Lookout Mountain in Golden. With the cityscape arrayed in front of him and pine trees on either side, he tried to think everything through. Katie probably wouldn't know he'd become a Super. How long could he keep something like that a secret?

Once she found out, she'd demand he reveal her weakness and start asking him for every other Super's weakness. He couldn't be a part of that. On the other hand, if he disappeared now, she'd have little trouble hunting him down. He didn't think she was above taking Juliet hostage and forcing him to help her.

He had a good job for the first time in his life. But how long could he go on with the charade? Sooner or later, Katie Siren would hunt down Farseer. It would be easy with so many people working for her. Then CJ would be stuck.

With no clear choices before him, he decided to go where he always went for advice.

"Forgive me, Father, for I have sinned."

Father Weaver looked at the confessional screen and said, "What have you done?"

"I think you know. I broke out of jail. And I helped Katie Siren take down Random Acts of Cowboy, although he shot me first, so I think it's probably fair. Still hurts, and I can't really lift things yet."

"CJ, I really…"

"I did those thousand and forty prayers you asked, plus every night I was in jail."

"Did you finish the ritual with Farseer?"

"Yes. But I'm going to have to lie about it to my new boss. Can I confess that before it happens? I probably better come back after."

"CJ, come outside."

CJ took a deep breath. He didn't like it when protocol broke down. He admired the crucifix and stained glass again.

"Listen, CJ, we talked about this before." Father Weaver put a hand on CJ's shoulder. "Pope Francis sent out a new decree. Everybody who is or works with a Supervillain is excommunicated."

"But Katie's not a Supervillain. She's making jobs and…"

"I'm sorry, CJ. There's nothing I can do, unless you go to the police and turn yourself in today."

"They'll put me away for life. I at least have to wait until…"

"No, CJ. No more waiting. No more schemes. You are a Super now, and you're working for a villain. I have no choice." He took his hand off and looked CJ in the eyes. "Colin John Leon De La Cruz, you are excommunicated from the Catholic Church. You can appeal to the Pope, but only after you demonstrate you have repented."

CJ heard sobbing in the back of the room. He turned to see red hair bowed with head in hands. "Delia?"

She looked up. The tears on her cheeks glistened in the low light. "Why, CJ?"

"She was here before you came in," Father Weaver said.

"Have you been here the whole time?" CJ asked. He walked toward her. "Delia, I've got a good job now. I can turn this all around." He looked back to the priest. "Right? This can be fixed?"

"Yes, but only if you turn yourself in." Father Weaver looked at the statue of Jesus and crossed himself. "Excuse me, please." He walked out the side door, leaving them alone.

CJ rushed to Delia, putting out his arms to hold her.

"No," she said. She wiped the tears off her cheeks and took a deep breath. "This is the end, CJ." She held out the pouch of gems Farseer gave him and dropped it in his hands. "I love you, but it's over now."

"It's just beginning," he said. "I'm a Super now. I have powers. I can finally take control and make things better."

"Better for who?"

"Better for people. For everybody."

"Not for me. You can't make this better."

She sobbed as she pushed the heavy wooden door open. Diffuse light from the overcast sky lit the cathedral for a few seconds, then faded.

CJ fell to the padded bench, tears filling both eyes. He raised both his hands. "Why? Why?"

20

CJ sold the gems. He returned his car to the dealer and bought something much more reasonable. He kept some cash in his wallet, and took the rest to Lexi's apartment. His heart broken, he stood at the door for a long while. He didn't want to face her. Everything she'd left him over had happened as she predicted. He was excommunicated, Delia left him, and the cops were after him. Worst of all, he was a horrible father. Now he had to leave; he couldn't even finish raising his daughter. He wanted to crawl under a rock and disappear. He wished never to face his ex-wife, now that he knew she was right to leave him. Still, he wouldn't leave until he at least did something for Juliet. He ignored the pain in his throat and knocked.

"Oh. It's you." Lexi had on her reading glasses. She didn't open the door more than three inches.

"I'm sorry for everything," CJ said. "I screwed up, a lot. Anyway, I might have to disappear for a while."

"On account of you're on the run from the police? Shocker."

"Thanks for making this easier." He shoved the wad of cash through the door. It was so big it forced the crack open wider.

"Where'd you get this?" she asked. Although the edge was off her voice.

"Does it matter?"

"Yes, but something tells me this is the last money you're ever going to give me."

"I hope not. But if you don't hear from me soon, it might be a while. Can

I talk to Juliet?"

Lexi shook her head, her eyes drooping.

CJ's emotions boiled over. "I just paid you twenty-thousand dollars. I think that entitles me to see Juliet without calling ahead to make a plan."

"You're going to break her heart. I always knew you would. I'd let you see her if she was here, but she's gone. She went to her friend's house after school. You can call her."

"I tried, her phone's off."

"That doesn't seem like her at all. Are you sure she just isn't avoiding your call?"

A dark fear came over him, imagining Katie already did something to Juliet. A higher voice from behind said, "I'm not. My battery died. I came home to get the charger."

CJ spun around. "I'm glad you're here." He reached down and gave her a big hug. "I need to talk to you. It's kind of an emergency."

"Okay." She waved over his shoulder. "I'll be back after dinner?"

"Yes," he said. "Let's eat. Anywhere you want."

"Mizuna?"

"Sure. I have a tie and jacket in my car." CJ grabbed her hand to go.

"Don't be silly," Lexi called. "That's a waste of money."

CJ ignored her. "You're worth it."

CJ didn't pay much attention as they ordered. The white tablecloth reminded him of Mirror Max. The food was great, but he didn't care. He put all his attention on his daughter.

"So, are you going away for a while? You're on the run from the police, right?"

"Yes. And I thought things were going to work out with my new job, but they aren't."

"You're with Katie Siren, right? That's a big step up." She lifted her phone, remembered it was dead, then stuck it deep in her pocket.

"I don't know how long I can stay there, actually. You see, something has happened." He tried to gauge from her expression how much he should tell her. Her black rimmed glasses made her look both frivolous and smart.

"What?" She didn't look eager, just curious and concerned.

"Can you keep a secret?"

She furrowed her brow. "I keep lots of secrets, remember?"

"Of course," he said. He patted her hand on the table, looking both ways before speaking quietly. "I'm a Super now."

"What?" She looked around, too. Seeing nobody interested in their conversation she whispered, "When did this happen? How did it happen?"

"Farseer. Well, she started it, but it finally happened today. Anyway, it's complicated. I don't want to keep working for Katie Siren with this power, it's…"

"I understand." He saw in her eyes she really did. It was easy to forget how smart and mature she'd become. More than anything else, he saw trust and admiration in her.

He just looked at her face. For so long he'd craved having anybody look up to him. Now, in the midst of such a mess, he couldn't enjoy it. "Thank you."

"You'll do the right thing."

The right thing? Did he even know what the right thing to do was? He watched her take a bite of duck in chestnut pudding. For so long he'd denied the titles of hero and villain. As long as he stayed normal, it didn't apply to him. He couldn't hide behind his shield of words anymore. For his daughter, the last person in the world who believed in him, he had to be a hero.

Whatever Katie planned now, he knew she would go too far if he helped her. She already threatened to turn him over to the police if he didn't do what she told him, though. As a normal, he had no choice, but he was a Super now. He didn't have to play the game by her rules. He could make his own. He would go to Katie Siren, find out her weakness and then tell her if she didn't leave him alone he would tell everybody. Maybe Juliet could help with that.

"Can you do me a favor?" he asked.

"Anything." She gave him a nice smile.

"I'm going to send you an e-mail later. If nothing happens, just delete it and never read it. I'm sure there is a way to password protect it or something, but I'm terrible with those things, so I'm just going to trust you on this one. If something happens to me, though, I need you to put it up on the Internet where everybody can see it. But do it anonymously so it can't be traced back to you. That's very important. People might come after you if they know it's you."

She nodded. "So you're using this information against somebody and you think they might hurt you?"

He let out a slow breath. "You know, there's such a thing as too smart."

She laughed. "I'll take care of your information."

"Thank you. I'd never put you in danger like this, but you're the only person I can trust. I'm so proud of you. You're the only thing I did right in this whole world. I wish things could be different. I wish…"

The waiter brought the bill.

WELL AFTER SUNSET, THE LIGHTS OF THE CITY LOOKED LIKE A MAGIC SPELL FROZEN in time through the windows of the Spire. CJ had his own condo there now. He hadn't bothered to buy furniture for it yet. Jasmine told him not to bring his old furniture. The walls were slightly off white with interesting architectural angles and big windows. CJ felt too anxious to sit in his empty place alone, so he went up to the command office.

He saw Katie there. She had a pearl dress on which shimmered green or pink in different lighting and matched a little hat she wore tipped to one side. "CJ, I'm glad to see you. How did that business with my thorn go?"

Before CJ could answer, understanding grew in his mind. Katie had three powers. The thing he'd been calling, "tactical genius" was actually two separate powers, one for tactics and the other for discerning the variables related to any situation. Her third power was a kind of intuition about normal people. She could easily measure their potential and skills. It didn't seem like a Super power, but coupled with the others, it made her capable of leading people to do almost anything she wanted. Her weakness was unexpected. She couldn't resist a challenge. If somebody suggested she do something, she would plot and scheme until it happened.

"Did you hear me?" she asked, turning toward him. "How did it go?"

CJ snapped out of the little spell drawing his attention. "I stopped him from messing up the warehouse deal. Also, I took his car. It has the computer the surveyors were using in the back. Although I left it parked in Globeville, so it might not still be there." He put Max's keys on the table.

She let out an exuberant laugh. He had to admit, her smile was attractive even now. "So the problem's fixed?"

"Maybe. It was a confusing conversation. If he shows up again, I'll have to have another talk with him and apply more force. I'm hoping he's seen sense, though."

"I prefer a definitive solution, but we'll see how it pans out." She checked her huge teardrop shaped pearl earring in a small mirror before she opened a communication line on one of the large screens in front of her. "Hello. I'll be there at nine or right after. I have a bit of business to finish up here first." She cut the line and turned back to CJ. "I gave all this to Jasmine, but I'll just tell you now that you're here. I put some feelers out and managed to locate Farseer. The little ferret's in California. Anyway, I figured the best way to do it is just for you to show up, that way we won't ruffle any of her feathers. I had somebody book you on a flight tomorrow morning."

CJ faked a smile. "Thanks." If nothing else, maybe he'd take that trip and just never come back. Maybe he could use his power to help Farseer. If Katie found her, it's a good bet more Supers were going to be onto her soon.

"I think this is going to work out marvelously." She walked toward the elevators. The door binged and slid open. She stopped and put a hand over her mouth. "You!"

CJ thought a herpetologist could have milked the venom in that single word.

"Hello." Mirror Max grinned and waved with one hand.

"I thought you said you took care of this," Katie shot a terrifying look at CJ.

"I thought I did." He stepped forward, positioning himself between Katie and MM.

Max pulled a gun. "Don't move." He walked toward Katie. "I don't know how long your powers will last before I get near enough to absorb hers again. I need them to work first and…"

"Katie, get back!" CJ yelled. "He's trying to find out your weakness."

Katie jumped behind a screen of monitors. She pushed a button on her remote. "Security, a man with a gun is…"

She went silent. The bullet hit one of the monitors, but she'd said enough. CJ, hands in the air, made a few small steps to intercept Mirror Max. "What are you hoping to accomplish here? When the guards show up, you'll be shot. You're only good move now is to run."

"Maybe," Max said, "But I don't have her tactical genius yet, so I can't be sure. Soon, though." He took several steps forward, trying to cover Katie with the gun through the spaces between desks. "Ah. There it is."

"What's happening," Katie asked. "Why do you want to kill me? I've never done anything to you."

"He has a hero-villain complex," CJ said.

"No, I'm over that." Max smiled. "Your weakness is so plebian, Katie. It must really bother you."

"How does he know my weakness? CJ did you forget to tell me something?" Real anger burned in her voice.

Guards began banging on the elevator door. "Let us in! It's jammed. Just shoot it open!"

"I'm sorry," CJ said. "I was going to tell you, but Max here interrupted."

"And I was going to leave after I got your weakness," Max said. "But now, thanks to your power, I realize there's no easy way out of here. If you hadn't called your attack dogs, we could have ended this peacefully."

"You think I'd just let you walk out of here knowing what you do about me?"

"I did. Now I realize that was a mistake, but I didn't have your powers to help me at the time."

"We get it," CJ said. "What are you going to do now?"

The men stopped shooting and started hammering on the elevator doors.

"Now I'm taking you both out of here at gunpoint, down the fire escape stairs."

"They will have it covered," Katie said.

"Then they will have to shoot you to get to me." Max waved with the gun.

Katie stood and straightened her dress. She stared daggers at CJ. The two of them headed toward the door painted to match the room so it wouldn't distract from the décor. When Katie looked at CJ, her eyes promised him a future of acute pain. She would hold him personally responsible for all of this. There wouldn't be anything he could say to fix it. If Mirror Max didn't kill him, Katie would.

21

As they moved slowly toward the door to the fire escape stairs, CJ re-evaluated his situation. He was on top of a skyscraper with two Supers. They both had Katie's powers of tactics, situational analysis, and understanding people's abilities. They'd both used that power on CJ before he became a Super, so they knew what he was capable of doing. CJ wasn't a genius, so he had no idea what the two of them would be planning. He was sure they were both planning and double planning, though. This was like a chess game between grand masters, and CJ was just one of the pieces.

The security men in the elevator were trying to break down the door, which would never work. CJ didn't know how Max had locked it, but it was obviously holding.

Mirror Max knew CJ's weakness, which CJ didn't know. He also knew Katie's weakness, which CJ did know. Katie could never resist a challenge. That was the only information CJ could use in this whole mess. However, he didn't know how far to take it.

CJ was not as tall as Max, but he felt reasonably confident he could win in a brawl if he wasn't still recovering from a chest wound. He'd go fifty-fifty odds on a fistfight, but CJ would only get one good hit before he hurt himself so bad it ended. Katie was a wild card in a struggle, because he had no idea what she was physically capable of doing.

CJ reached the door first. Katie kept stalling and moving to the side. She obviously wanted Max to get near CJ and lose her power, so she'd have the advantage. Max, of course, was now too smart to fall for something so simple. He kept a good amount of distance away, with Katie in the middle.

CJ had his hands in his pockets. He touched his Swiss army knife, but knew better than to think it would be any help against somebody with a gun.

"Stop stalling or I'll just shoot you now!" Max made a show of aiming for CJ's head.

"Sorry," CJ said with his hands up. "But I'm still recovering from a bullet wound, so I doubt I will be able to walk down forty flights of stairs without passing out." He was already tired, so it wasn't a lie. He doubted he could lie to these two. Now that he was a Super, they couldn't use their power to know his abilities anymore. That only worked on normals. However, they'd both scanned him with it before he made the change.

"We don't have time to wait for you," Max said. "Since she set off the siren, security will call the police. We can't wait for that."

"The only good move is to leave him here," Katie said. "Then we can travel faster down the stairs. But since I'm in heels, it's still going to take a while."

"We already wasted too much time talking about it." Max's eyes darted around the room, tallying assets and making a new plan. "It'll have to be the elevator. First, we need to secure this door. Put that cabinet in front of it."

CJ walked over to the filing shelf along the wall next to the door. It was six feet tall and four drawers wide, full of paper. He tried to push it, but only managed to get it a few feet before exhaustion and pain in his chest forced him to stop. "I can't."

"Stupid bullet wound," Max said.

"I've been saying that a lot lately." CJ leaned against the metal side of the furniture, letting the metal cool his forehead. He wished he had his suit on now. It was looking more and more like he would die before this ended, and he wanted to die in a nice suit. Maybe they'd bury him in it at least. It didn't matter, though, because he was going to hell for sure now. Whether he died today or in forty years didn't make any difference. He couldn't confess his sins and he couldn't get last rights. The thought depressed him. He half hoped Max would just shoot him. At least that way people would know he died fighting Supers.

"Help him." Max waved the pistol at Katie. She looked at her dress and heels, clearly aghast at the suggestion. CJ wondered why people always used guns like pointers. It really didn't make sense.

With Katie on the far side, CJ pushed again. Three heaves later, they managed to have the files in front of the door. CJ fell to the floor, gasping for breath and seeing stars.

"Now go let the security men out of the elevator." Max's eyes were wild now. Was his genius turning to madness? Was Katie's mind too much for Max's brain to hold, despite the super power?

Katie walked toward the elevator. "Stop! Not you, obviously."

CJ used one of the metal drawer handles to pull himself up, gasping for breath. It hurt more than anything he'd ever felt. Although it probably hurt more when he woke up in the hospital, he had strong painkillers to help then. He suspected he'd made the wound worse and it would take longer to heal now. He pretended to be out of breath still, hoping to stall. He still hadn't figured out who he wanted to win in this battle of wits.

If he helped Katie win, she might trust him again, but then he'd have to tell her her weakness and help her defeat all the other Supers. He didn't know what Mirror Max wanted. His best guess was that Max hoped to get close to Katie and copy her powers, and then use them to make a lot of money or something. If Max won, he wouldn't want CJ around, meaning CJ would be left behind. Then Katie would still use him, or possibly just kill him.

CJ crept toward the elevator, making a show of coughing every few steps. Maybe when he let the guards out, he could take the elevator down and escape.

When he reached the elevator, CJ found an electrical panel had been torn open and several wires were pulled out. A small circuit board with a computer chip and several other electrical parts CJ couldn't identify was spliced into two of the wires. Clearly, this circuit was responsible for holding the door closed.

"Hold on," CJ called through the door, "I'll let you out."

"What's happening? Is Katie safe?"

CJ didn't answer them. He turned to Mirror Max, "Where'd you get this? You obviously didn't build it."

"Actually, I didn't. I have a friend who built it for me. He's a genius, too."

"Why didn't you just get his genius powers, then?"

"He wouldn't let me. But he gave me that and told me Katie would be here, so it's just as good."

So there was another player in this game. CJ didn't know whom, but that person knew better than to let Max near. Did that Super know about CJ's power? Why would he or she do all this for Max? CJ had been in this business long enough to know it wasn't a coincidence. Somebody wanted Max up here. CJ picked the small green card up and tilted it gently. "How do I turn it off?"

"Just disconnect it from the wires."

CJ pulled. The alligator clips let go. The door binged opened an inch.

"Go, go!" Somebody inside the elevator yelled.

Another said, "It's still stuck. We bent it so it will only open part way."

After a short commotion the first said, "Then force it open."

When three men emerged, carrying machine guns of various sizes and types, CJ pointed to Mirror Max. "Over there. He's got her hostage." The three men fanned out, pointing their guns at Max, who now had one arm around Katie's neck with the gun pointing at her head.

"I think you all know how this is going to go," Max said calmly. "Put your guns down and your hands up."

CJ looked at the mangled elevator door. It would never close. The dumb machine kept trying to slide it open and closed in turns, with an annoying click that never stopped. He could at least go in there to hide from gunfire. With both the exits blocked, this whole problem was about to escalate. Max now had to keep five hostages in check using one gun. There were machine guns in the mix. So there was a good chance things were about to get prolonged and bloody.

How could it have devolved into this? With two geniuses in the room, the whole thing still ended with a gun and a hostage? Shouldn't they just stare into each other's eyes and have a complicated conversation where they each thrust and parry their ideas until they both knew who would win, then shake hands and walk away? It turned out the game was the same whether you were a corporation mogul or a street punk looking to score a bank job.

"You, too, Probe-boy."

Probe-boy? CJ peeked around the corner. Mirror Max looked right at him. "Get out here and join the others."

Probe-boy? CJ felt slandered to the depths of his soul. Was that really how Max and Katie saw him? He was just another science instrument they could use? More than anything else, it was the least cool Super name he'd ever heard. CJ prayed it wouldn't catch on. These things had a way of becoming permanent. Usually Supers make their own name and logo, but CJ had been too preoccupied. He'd been excommunicated, lost his girlfriend, and on the run from the police. When would he have time to think up a name and logo? It was monumentally unfair. If it stuck somehow, CJ would have to seek vengeance in the form of Max in great pain.

"Now!"

CJ put his hands up and came around the corner. He continued to hobble, pretending to be in pain. When he joined the security guards, all standing in a line, with his hands up, he said, "That's not my name."

The woman next to him with her hands up grunted a laugh. "Probe-boy.

Classic."

"That's NOT my name," CJ said through gritted teeth. Of course, the guard was a normal, so CJ's power gave him absolutely no information about her.

"It is now." She snickered, along with the others with her. CJ felt murderous rage rising inside him. It made his chest hurt.

"Hey, Katie Siren," CJ said, "I bet you can't find a way to distract Max."

She looked at him for a second, squinted her eyes, then stomped a stiletto heel into Max's foot.

"Aaargh!" Max moved back. Katie spun around, grabbing for the gun. The security guards all leaped on their machine guns. CJ bolted for the elevator. Max recovered. "Freeze!" He had the gun leveled at Katie's chest.

CJ stopped, one foot away from the steel-walled safety chamber. The guards were all in various kneeling postures.

The floor and windows vibrated. CJ looked back at the elevator. The security crew were out here, so it couldn't be them. They all looked at each other again, beginning to get up with their hands raised. Katie kept calm, maintaining her composure. If there hadn't been a gun involved, people might just think she was being interviewed by Max to promote her newest line of cosmetics.

A few seconds later, it happened again.

"What is that?" the woman next to CJ asked. The guard by her shrugged.

"My ride!" Max had a wide grin, like his racehorse had just won him a million bucks. "You didn't think I'd come here without some kind of escape plan, did you?"

"The other genius," CJ said, snapping his fingers.

"Of course."

Bright lights flooded the buildings outside the Spire. A huge machine with metal legs two-hundred feet high stomped into view, rattling all the computers and screens. It turned, training searchlights on the windows of the Spire, making it impossible to see any details. Small drones hovered around it like worker bees.

CJ jumped into the elevator and curled up on the floor, by the wall.

The windows shattered, thrusting glass shards in every direction. Then a missile exploded.

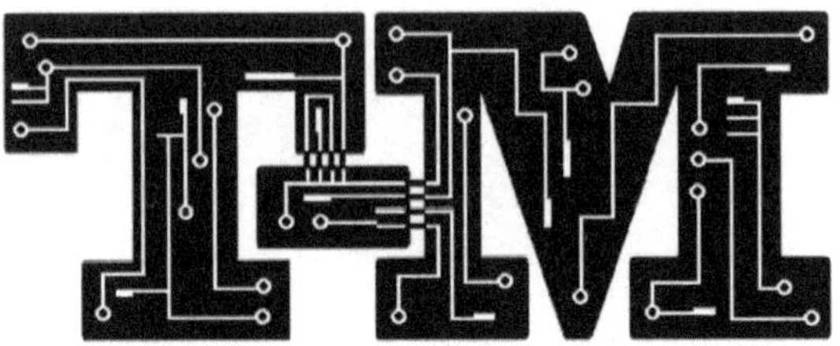

22

CJ coughed. As he sat up, fearful of another attack, dust fell from his hair and clothes. He stood, expecting another blast. When nothing came, he poked his head out. Cool night wind blew through the now open room. He couldn't see much except the lights of the giant machine making cones in the settling dust. He squeezed out the opening and stepped forward, surveying the room.

All the desks and computers from the middle of the office sat in heaps along the sides and back of the room where the explosion had thrown them. Small fires crackled around the room, but it was hard to hear over the roaring of engines right outside the building. Luckily, CJ had covered his ears as part of covering his head when he jumped to the ground. Otherwise, he'd probably be deaf now.

Katie and Max weren't so lucky. Their bodies lay twisted in the heap of scrap along the wall next to the elevator. The security guards were buried in the mess. For an instant CJ regretted that he'd never learn his weakness from Max, then he felt guilty for thinking it. Katie's legs twisted so one of her expensive shoes stuck up at a strange angle from the wreckage.

The behemoth machine stood motionless outside the shattered windows like a dragon searching for new prey. CJ thought about hiding again, but it would be no use. If the operator wanted him dead, CJ would die. His eyes eventually adjusted to the light, so he could see the war vehicle. Unpainted steel plating on the outside, the cockpit looked like an airplane nose mounted over a huge network of engines. One of the giant arms had a massive claw. The other had a .50-caliber machine gun hand with a flamethrower and grenade launcher mounted above it. Over each shoulder, a large array of missiles waited in boxes of stacked launch tubes.

Where had this thing come from? It had to be close, where had it been hidden in the city? CJ remembered his trip to Globeville to meet Max. He'd seen pieces of airplane fuselage outside a warehouse there.

The nose of the titanic machine moved forward and settled on the edge of the now open wall. Pieces of concrete broke and fell away as the heavy device strained the building's structure. A door opened and a man stepped out.

Wrapped from neck to foot in Kevlar, the outside of the suit had wires and circuitry running up and down the arms, legs, and body. Small LED lights blinked on and off in seemingly random patterns all over the outfit. His head had a strange helmet with various lenses and sensors sticking out in funny places. Beneath that, his hair stuck out. He looked like a scientist from the distant future stepping out of a time machine.

CJ walked toward him, squinting to make out details in the flood of light. The front of the outfit had a blocky 'TM' logo with stylized circuitry lit from behind. The color slowly cycled through the entire spectrum.

The man raised his hand. "We meet again, CJ." He had to speak loud to be heard over the engines.

Again? Did CJ know this guy? TM… Travis Mueller. This was the first of Farseer's people to become a Super. He'd punched Rack in the face. "Hello, Travis. I think you accidentally blasted the guy you were here to pick up."

Travis smiled with half his mouth. "You remember me. It wasn't an accident. I had to get rid of Katie, she was the only one smart enough to stop me. Max would have been smart enough if I let him get near me."

"You're the one who made the electronic override lock for the elevator."

"Of course."

CJ stepped closer. All at once, he knew Travis was a level four Super. All his powers centered around programming, engineering, and technology. It turned out his genius was natural, not part of the Super mix at all. He also knew Travis' weakness: women. CJ had to bite his lip to not laugh aloud at the cliché. The nerd couldn't resist attention from anyone of the opposite gender.

"You made a logo out of your own initials?" Some heroes adapted their name, like Katie and Max. A few just kept their name, but they usually didn't make a logo.

"No. I have a Super moniker. I'm the *Tech-Monger*."

CJ glanced at the metal monstrosity again and shuddered. "That's really amazing." He hoped Travis didn't know he was a Super.

"Max told me you have a very useful power, too."

Crap. "Yeah?"

"He said you can tell a Super's weakness just by looking at them."

CJ wanted to deny it, but he knew from sad experience that lying to geniuses wouldn't work. From the looks of this room, lying to Travis was signing his own death warrant. "He's right. He had my power for a while. Although I don't know if *every* Super has a weakness."

"So you can tell my weakness already, right?"

CJ let out a deep breath. "Yes."

"I think I could use a guy like you. I'm bound to draw a lot of unwanted attention from Superheroes. You care to team up?"

At least a dozen missiles on the rack mounted above the behemoth's shoulder were pointed at CJ as they spoke. *Thou shalt not lie.* He didn't really have much of a choice. If he refused, Travis would kill him just like Katie to keep him from being a threat. "Of course. That sounds great! You probably have some big plans."

"I do. First, I'm going to get some money. Then I'm going to set up shop somewhere remote. I have some solid ideas for huge improvements in cell-phone technology. I'm thinking augmented reality glasses that wrap around and scan the user's hands and eyes for control signals. Also, I want to look into 4-D movies. I have a million ideas people will love."

"Are you going to use investors? You'll need a lot of capitol up front."

CJ didn't know much about business, but he'd picked a few things up the last couple of weeks working for Katie.

"No. I'm just going to knock over a few banks here in Denver."

CJ shook his head gently. "With this giant exo-armor vehicle thing, if you start stealing money, you're bound to draw out the Control Crew. This is just the kind of thing they love. High profile. Having blasted Katie and Max, you'll be lucky if they only send one now. If you start hitting banks, they'll bring the whole team."

"You're saying I should keep a low profile and work from inside the system?"

"Yes. Tell them Max was an accident. Tell them you took out Katie because she's a villain and you want to be a Superhero. Then you can build your stuff and make billions. They'll probably even help promote your work."

"Interesting," Travis said. "So you're in?"

"Yes." CJ didn't want to. He knew where this would lead. He'd gotten in way over his head, but if Travis would listen to reason, maybe he could make a go of it. At this point, he knew it really didn't matter anymore. He was going to hell, so all he really wanted was to stay alive and out of jail as long as possible, postponing the inevitable judgment.

"In that case, I'm going to need a show of faith from you," Travis said.

"You can't resist women." CJ stepped forward and patted Travis on the shoulder sympathetically. "In a way, I guess they are all our weakness. You've got it worse though. Much worse."

"That doesn't make any sense," Travis said. He marched back into the control center for the machine. "That has nothing to do with my powers."

CJ smiled and followed him in. "Tech guy can't handle females? Oh, it makes perfect sense. And it proves God has a sense of humor."

"So where did you get the money for this thing?" CJ asked. He was strapped into a chair. The head of the machine bobbed and lurched as it walked through the city, smashing roads as it went. The motion gave CJ a headache, as the strap holding him into the chair hurt his chest. There were tools and gadgets all over the place. Everything from strange batteries with wires sticking out one end to a crowbar. They all had special straps or clamps holding them firmly in place as the jerky robot lumbered around.

"I work in military research. I just diverted government funds and supplies."

"That explains the drones."

"Those we already had built, I just reprogrammed them." Travis stood on a platform in the middle of three gyroscopes. Sensors in his suit sent control signals to the huge vehicle, which moved to copy his actions. "You know, when I get some time, I think I'm going to re-do the controls for this craft. I thought it would be cool to have it mimic my movements, but frankly, it's exhausting. I'm not used to this kind of fine motor control sustained over time."

"That's why a lot of people don't like video games that use cameras." CJ looked out the front window to see where they were going. It wasn't Globeville. They were heading southeast. "They'd rather use a controller so they can sit while they play."

"I agree with them now. Also, I think I need gyroscopes to stabilize the control room and not just the control platform."

CJ didn't answer, trying to keep from puking when the whole thing lurched to the side. "Where are we going?"

"Three-hundred forty, Colfax Avenue."

"That's by the state capital, right?"

Travis flashed him a quick smile. "Yep."

"The U.S. Mint." CJ faked a smile, but he felt a pit in his stomach. He already knew he was up for life if they ever caught him. So it didn't really matter anymore. Still, as amazing as Travis's walker was, it would never be good enough to withstand a full-scale attack from the government.

"I don't have time to wait for investors." Travis pivoted the machine. Then he lowered his hands. Giant hydraulics in the legs brought the machine down. It still towered high above the three-story government building. "Do you know where in this place they keep the cash?"

CJ shook his head.

Travis took one hand out of a control glove and typed into a tablet fastened to his left forearm. The drones all took off, scanning the building. Travis put his hand back in the glove. As the rings spun around him, Travis leaned forward and moved his hand around. The walker's claws reached

UNITED STATES MINT

forward and demolished the roof and upper floors of the building.

Travis methodically tore the place apart for about five minutes. A few guards ran outside and opened fire with machine guns. It didn't do anything to the machine, of course.

When one of them showed up with a bazooka, Travis turned the other hand that way and blasted a stream of fire out of the flamethrower. The missile blew up in the tube.

Travis uncovered a loading dock where several security trucks parked. He stacked two up, grabbed them with the big claw, then stomped off in the other direction. The interior of the control room was so well insulated, CJ couldn't hear much of anything outside. He could barely even hear the exploding bazooka.

"This should be enough cash to get us started," Travis said.

"It's definitely enough to retire on." CJ didn't dare hope Travis would see the wisdom in those words. "But Denver's mint only makes coins. How can you spend it?"

"You're funny. There's cash in these trucks, too. But I'm only taking dollar coins."

"Where to now?"

"Time to get out of sight."

Numerous helicopters flew over Denver now. Cops and news trucks were coming out all over the city. "Something tells me they aren't going to lose sight of this thing."

"Funny you should say that. Push the blue button on the console next to you, please. I can activate it from here, but it's a pain."

CJ scanned the panel of controls. The blue button was under a home-made sticker label that said *Camouflage*. How was that possible? Could this machine make itself look like a building? CJ pushed the button.

The lights went out. The room stopped bobbing and began to move in slower, less-jerky motions. They were in Globeville now. Travis brought the machine to a stop, collapsing the legs and dropping them down so the control room was only a hundred feet above the ground. Then it slowly tipped on its side and lay down. CJ was lying on his back in the chair when it finally set down on the ground.

The rings orbiting Travis had tilted as they dropped. Now they slowed.

"It's not a perfect system, but it uses scanners and projectors to make the machine body look like whatever's behind it. It won't work at close range, but in this form, it looks like a warehouse.

CJ pushed the release button and rubbed his chest before he stood up.

"I think this is going to work out well," Travis said. "You know a lot of things I don't."

"But you didn't take my advice."

"No, but I can imagine situations where I might. Anyway, come meet the rest of my men. I'm promoting you to be my right-hand man. You're my number one assistant."

"Great."

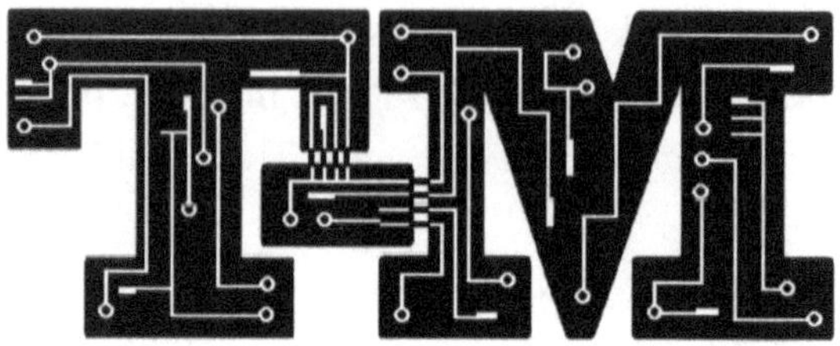

23

"So you can't see his weakness yet?" Travis watched the video footage of a blue and gold clad man flying through the air, patrolling the skies of Colorado.

"No, I have to actually get close," CJ said.

"We can arrange that." Travis slapped CJ on the back.

Under his breath, CJ muttered, "Wonderful. I always wanted to be ten feet away from Awesoman while I'm working for a psychopath."

The television reporter said, "Hundreds of eye witnesses report seeing a giant robot attack the Spire just two nights ago. Security footage has been patched together to create this image." An impressive and accurate picture of the giant walker came on the screen. "The Control Crew sent Awesoman to Denver the next day. I talked to many of Denver's citizens. Most of them said things similar to this man."

A large man with a beard and motorcycle t-shirt came on. He said, "We've had a [beep]-storm of Superheroes and villains taking over this city one after another for too long now. I'm glad somebody finally took notice and stepped in to do something about it."

"Once you know his weakness, it will be easy to take him out," Travis said.

CJ nodded. The screen changed back to the reporter. In the corner was a picture of Awesoman's logo. A large "A" shape with the bar across the middle replaced by the double-C cross of the Control Crew. All the Control

Crew members incorporated the group symbol into their personal logos. "At least they only sent one so far. He's one of the best though. I think he's at least level six."

"It doesn't matter if he's level two-hundred and six if he has a weakness. And once we use it against him, he'll be no better than Shooting Star, babbling incoherently in the loony-bin." Travis moved to a table full of what looked like a jumble of computers and wires to CJ, and looked at Denver on Google Earth.

"Yeah." CJ felt a pang of guilt. He hadn't shot SS with the dart. The sidekick had recovered. None of them had known what the long-term effects of Farseer's drug would be. It just felt wrong leaving somebody in such a state. Death seemed more merciful. No wonder Tech-Monger assumed CJ was a villain who wanted to bring down Awesoman and the rest of the Control Crew. Based on his track record alone, CJ looked like a hardened criminal.

No doubt, Father Weaver thought the same thing. Delia was a mystery, though. She looked impressed when she heard CJ took out Shooting Star. It didn't matter now. Once he was excommunicated, she wanted nothing to do with him.

CJ thought of Juliet and choked up. She would find all of this out, if she didn't know already. Deep down, he wanted to hope she would understand. He wasn't a villain. He was just a regular guy doing his job. She knew that, right?

He caught himself. Everything changed when he became a Super. He'd always held Supers up to a different standard than normals. The way normals judged Supers had always been wrong. They weren't just heroes and villains. There was a wide spectrum of complex motivations and internal struggles. CJ always saw them like a metaphysical conversation about power and meaning. They exemplified certain aspects of life and humanity.

Now he'd become one, and he couldn't see himself as something larger than life. Sure, he had powers, but they didn't make him feel Super. He still felt like a regular guy. And if he was just a normal person with powers, what did that make all the other Supers?

As he watched Awesoman flying around above the city, conspicuously doubling back so the helicopter camera could get several good shots, CJ didn't know what he was. He couldn't fly. He wasn't bullet proof. It didn't matter what his weakness was, because he could be taken out with a spoon thrown by somebody like Awesoman.

In the grand scheme of things, his power was strategically very valuable. He was coming to understand that. Whichever Super had CJ on their side would always have a big advantage over any other Supers. However, he would never be the main player. He would always be the wingman. If he worked with a hero, he'd be the sidekick. If he worked for a villain, he'd always be thug number one.

"There!" Tech-Monger said, pointing to the screen.

"Sports Authority Field at Mile High?" CJ pushed his hands deep in his pockets and walked over. "What about it?"

"That's where we'll draw Awesoman out, so you can figure out his weakness."

"Why there?"

TM stood up and walked around the table to an open area filled with a plethora of electronic parts and equipment CJ couldn't identify. He plugged several things into each other, then ran a wire from a blue circuit board to one of the USB ports in the back of the computer. He came back around the front and typed gibberish, which must have been program code. "I'm not going myself, of course. That would be stupid. But I'll send some bait. A robot that looks like me, but has a camera and speaker, kind of like a mobile video chat unit. I'll make it look like an exo-suit, but much smaller and with almost no real functions."

TM snapped his fingers. "A jet pack! That'll grab A-man's attention. Anyway, you hide out at the football arena. I'll draw him to you. When he lands, I'll keep him busy with stupid banter, like he's probably used to from the villains he deals with. You get a read on him and then just stay out of sight. When it devolves to violence, which it inevitably will, he'll bust up the bait robot and fly away. Easy."

IT DIDN'T GO DOWN LIKE THAT.

CJ had a terrible time breaking into the locked stadium. They postponed the plan so he could get in the next day with the cleaning crew. TM said it was better anyway, and spent the day hacking into the controls for the stadium. By the time evening rolled around, because Tech-Monger insisted it had to go down at night, CJ was hungry, bored, and sore. There was nowhere to get comfortable, and his chest ached.

When night finally came, TM turned on all the stadium lights remotely. Then he sent the machine up into the sky, shooting fireworks out of a mock rocket-launcher pack over the shoulders of the new robot. It looked a lot like his much bigger one that had been all over the news, except only ten feet tall. He said, "Awesoman won't even notice or care about the size difference."

CJ couldn't believe it. "The real one's twenty times bigger!"

"Watch. You'll see."

Sure enough, Awesoman didn't even hesitate. He chased the bot straight back to Mile High. The over-illumination of an empty stadium didn't give the Super pause either.

As the metal descended, its rocket pack leaving two big burn marks on the grass, Awesoman landed gracefully in front of it. He had a bright blue costume with a wispy cape. The gold *A* logo on his chest was bigger on the back of the cape. He had matching gold boots and a gold belt to give the costume a touch of class.

Awesoman faced away from CJ, pointing at the emblem on the robot's chest plate. "What's TM stand for?"

"What's it to you?" the speakers in the robot's head buzzed because they were set to such high volume.

CJ tried to figure out Awesoman's powers and weakness, but the Super was almost on the fifty-yard line. So CJ came out from behind the wall in the end zone. He felt exposed with so much light and so much open grass between him and the blue and gold Super. He didn't see any other way, so he

just walked forward, hoping the robot would keep those blue eyes pointed in the other direction.

"I like to know the name of the villains I take out," Awesoman said.

"You're so sure you'll take me out?"

"Please," the Super scoffed. He put his fists on his hips, accentuating his oversized physique. "I could take you out blindfolded with both hands tied behind my back."

"Care to try?"

"Look, if you don't want to tell me your name, that's fine. Most of your type are attention gluts, and want the news to splash it all over the place for two days after they go down. It's like the Supervillain consolation prize."

CJ walked forward in silence, staring at the back of Awesoman's blond hair. He kept track of the yard-line markers on the ground. It would be useful to know exactly how close he had to be to use his powers. He was tempted to run, but suppressed the urge.

The robot lifted its machine gun arm. "The consolation prize this time will go to you, Ass-man."

The sound of helicopters approaching made everything more stressful. News people would have cameras. The police would have guns. Either way, CJ didn't want to be seen as part of this exchange. He began to jog forward past the twenty-yard line, then to the thirty.

"Come on, it's not like I've never heard that one before. Aren't you supposed to be some kind of…" Awesoman twisted around. "Hey!"

CJ clamped his jaw and stared down at the ground. He didn't want this guy getting a good look at him. He slowed a little, but kept walking forward.

"Stop right there. Who are you?"

Helicopters crested the ridge. CJ didn't stop moving forward. Forty-yard line.

Light, brighter than the stadium's halogens, blossomed as a missile exploded on Awesoman right after a spray of machinegun fire tore a trench through the fake grass near CJ's feet. Awesoman, unhurt, turned back toward the robot.

"Bring it on!" the speakers rattled with the loud voice.

CJ felt his powers kick in when he crossed the Forty-three yard line, about fifteen feet from Awesoman. In a streak of blue, the Control Crewman leaped at the robot.

Two more missiles exploded, making it impossible for anybody to see or hear what was happening amidst the fire and smoke.

CJ ran. He didn't head back to the end zone. He went toward the closest bleachers. Artillery sounds behind him went on for a few more seconds before it stopped. When CJ made it to the benches, he jumped over the little wall and tucked himself down behind it, gasping for breath. His chest burned. He knew the concrete barrier would be nothing against Awesoman if the Super found him.

"Don't make the mistake of thinking you've stopped me!" Tech-Monger's voice came through the stadium speakers so loud they could hear it a mile away in the city. "This was just a brief introduction. Next time we meet, you die!"

Despite everything, CJ felt glad Travis had avoided the urge to give an evil laugh. It wasn't just a joke among villains—it was tacky. Awesoman yelled something, but CJ couldn't hear it over the din. The cold concrete leeched heat from CJ's wound. He panted, knowing if Awesoman found him here, he would be helpless. Even knowing the Super's weakness wouldn't save him.

The helicopter kept circling above. At some point, Awesoman left, but CJ didn't see it. When two more helicopters joined the scene, CJ knew he would be caught if he didn't move soon. They would be sending detectives and cops to investigate what was left of the rubble.

Taking great care, CJ rolled. He stayed close to the wall and crawled to the nearest opening. Once he entered the shadow of the blinding lights, the stadium speakers boomed again. "I am Tech-Monger. I will destroy Awesoman."

He shook his head as he worked his way back into the dark halls past closed concession stands toward the service door. Travis should've kept his mouth shut. It never paid to call out a Super.

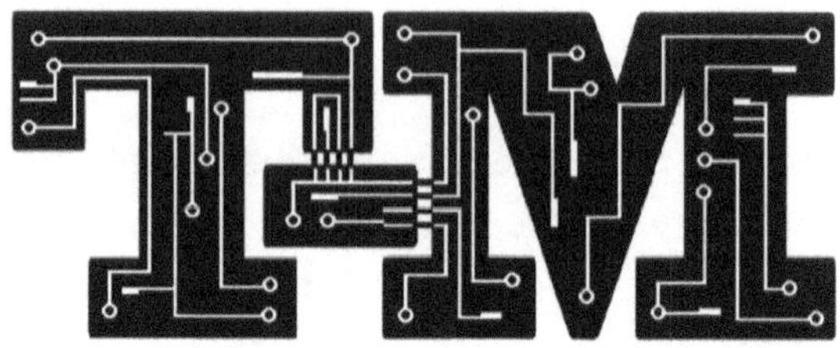

24

CJ sat in a coffee shop, eating a bagel. Out the window, a car with red and blue flashing lights occasionally sped by. Several police helicopters joined the news ones, flying in large circles around Mile High Stadium.

Despite being chilled, CJ ditched the hoodie as he left the stadium. Now he had on a bright orange t-shirt with a blue Broncos logo on the front. It reminded him of a Super logo. He'd learned this strategy from Farseer. Most people hiding will choose black and stick to the shadows. If you are wearing bright orange and sitting in plain sight by a window, they won't even look twice. The thought made him miss Farseer and George. He wished that gig could have gone on for a decade or more.

The barista had the television turned to the news. She watched it with her back to CJ. The first helicopter on the scene had distant, blurry footage of the final battle. It showed Awesoman looking at CJ before a missile blasted him from behind. They kept the camera on the battle at the time. Now they were blowing up the shot of CJ running from the mayhem. The reporter said, "The question on everybody's mind tonight is, who is this man? Was he part of Tech-Monger's attack on Awesoman? Was he purposefully distracting the Superhero? Or is this Tech-Monger, controlling the robot remotely? Or was he just some deranged person too dumb to stay out of the way?"

Luckily, they only had pixelated and shaky footage of CJ's head with the hood up. They wouldn't be able to identify him from it. He knew if they had anything better, they'd be showing it.

She continued, "Police are asking anybody with information about this man to come forward. Any information will help. Awesoman is patrolling the skies, looking for clues."

CJ ran his hand through his hair as his phone buzzed. The message from TM said, *Are you okay? Do you need me to come and get you?*

CJ smiled. Travis was a megalomaniac, no doubt. Even by CJ's definition, he was a villain. Still, CJ liked that somebody cared enough to check up on him. So many times, he had to take off when Supers came in to take out his employer. None of them had been concerned about what happened to CJ. Well, except Farseer. Maybe this was an aspect of being the right-hand man to a Super. Supers didn't keep track of their henchmen, but they cared about their sidekicks.

CJ typed, *I'm okay. I'll get back after the heat's off.*

He texted his daughter and Delia. Juliet responded and they chatted via text for an hour. The phone Katie gave him was great. He wondered how long the service would last before somebody at the company realized he was still using it and cancelled it; or worse, used it to track him down. He'd get a new one from TM soon.

Juliet texted, *So, was that you on the news with Awesoman?*

He didn't want to admit to it in print. Things like that had a tendency to come back and bite people. He wrote, *Only somebody stupid would do that.*

She'd know what he meant.

"That's his weakness?" Travis swiveled on his chair and looked CJ straight in the face. He had a grin that etched deep lines in both cheeks. "Seriously?"

CJ shrugged. "He's a level six. Two for flying, Two for strength, and Two for invulnerable skin."

"But that doesn't make any sense," Travis said. He still had a maniacal expression. "How could that even hurt him if he's bulletproof and fire proof?"

"I don't know how it works," CJ said. "Chances are he doesn't know how it works either, if he knows about it at all. So are you going to build something to exploit his weakness?"

"No." TM turned back to his computer and typed.

"No?" CJ didn't like the answer. "You're not going to take him out?"

"Oh, I am. Or, more to the point, you are. But we don't want to let on that we know his weakness. With that video footage of you, if we just up and take him out, people will easily figure out what you can do. We don't want anybody figuring out your power, it's too valuable."

CJ agreed emphatically. "Then how?"

"It has to look like an accident." He pulled up a picture of the robot Awesoman recently destroyed and photoshopped in a picture of CJ.

"You're making me an exo-suit?"

"Jetpack, really. But this time, you bait him here." On the next screen, TM brought up a map. He pointed north of Denver.

"Longmont?"

"Lots of farms and open spaces."

"HOW DID YOU BUILD IT SO FAST?" CJ LOOKED AT THE METAL SUIT IN AWE. Tech-Monger had built in weeks what researchers had failed to produce in decades. Attached to the huge jetpack were legs, each with two fins pointing out to the sides.

Tech-Monger handed him a helmet with a clear, pointed faceplate that reminded CJ of a bird. "I used to build drones. Adapting this was child's play."

CJ rubbed his chest. As much as he knew this wasn't safe, he really wanted to fly in this machine. "You set everything else up?"

"Of course. I built a map into the helmet that will direct you to the exact right place."

CJ pulled the helmet on and took a deep breath. "Let's do this."

"Wow!" CJ's body vibrated as the jets lifted him from the ground. His chest hurt in a dull way. The thrill of flying more than compensated for the discomfort.

His feet were locked together at the ankles. He moved them to steer. By shifting left or right, the suit turned to follow. He went up or down the same way. He rose into the clear, afternoon sky and began making a wide circle over the city. "I could get used to this."

"No sign of Awesoman?" He heard Tech-Monger through the speakers in his helmet.

"Not yet."

"He'll be there soon. After another circle, you should probably head north. He can fly faster, so you'll want a good lead."

CJ zigzagged over the busiest parts of downtown, smiling when people looked up and pointed. He watched his shadow fall over buildings and pedestrians. Deep down, he wished his power had been flying. The sense of freedom and exhilaration filled him. He was tempted to just fly away with the suit and never come back. He could go somewhere tropical where there was no Tech-Monger or Awesoman. The only problem was, there wouldn't be any Juliet or Delia either. Besides, he had no idea how to refuel this thing, and something told him Travis could track him to the end of the Earth.

CJ turned north, catching a bit of uprising air, and lurching on his way out of town. From high up, roads and fields created a texture. When he wasn't in it, Denver didn't seem like a very big place.

The helmet signaled TM's equipment sensing the Super. Travis's voice came through the com. "He's on your trail. Nothing fancy now, just follow the plan."

"Roger." CJ rolled his eyes at himself.

He couldn't look back to see Awesoman. CJ had no idea how close the Super was. The suit only had one readout, a map showing a red dot for CJ

and a red dot for the target location. CJ had a throttle in one hand to manually increase or decrease the output of the jetpack. He cranked it up to maximum and steered lower.

"How close is he now?" CJ asked. The fuel burning above him was so loud he wondered if TM even heard him.

There was some static on the line. "He's about two hundred yards and closing. You should make it at this rate, but it's going to be close."

CJ muttered. "Of course." Why was it always so close?

All the enjoyment of flying drained away as CJ split his attention between watching the red dots on the map come together and scanning the ground for the target. As usual, Tech-Monger did his work alone, so CJ hadn't actually seen the place yet.

"Can you turn off that beeping?"

"No, sorry. Didn't think of that."

"What does it look like, anyway?" CJ was getting close to treetops now, going way too fast to stop. He didn't want to slow down and get caught, of course. Awesoman would tear this jetpack apart in two seconds. On the other hand, he had to land soon, and that necessitated slowing down."

"How close now?" Worry crept into CJ's voice.

"He's about fifty yards behind you. Just drop between the trees in the main corridor, and you should see it soon."

CJ was going too fast to make any sense out of the apple trees ahead of him. He eased up on the throttle, aiming down even more. He flew too close for comfort. The orchard rows had one channel wider than the others. He wouldn't have any room to maneuver. One stray branch would bring him to a fiery end. Awesoman wouldn't have any such concerns.

As CJ plunged into a fast moving trench beneath the leafy canopy, a large metal shed appeared ahead of him. At this speed, he'd be there in seconds.

"Just go into the box?"

"It will close automatically."

"But I have to slow down first and…" Too late to explain, CJ slid the throttle back with his thumb. He knew Awesoman would catch him soon, but he had no choice. If he hit that vault going full speed, he'd be a flaming ball of rocket fuel and do the Super's work for him.

CJ killed the engines. When he went past the zero point on the throttle, flaps opened on the sides of the pack, then a parachute. His chest hurt at the sudden yanking back. He knew he was doomed now. Awesoman would grab that chute and use the entire jetpack as a bolo, tossing CJ into a large tree trunk and saving the police the trouble of finding him.

All at once, the vault door slammed behind him and CJ found himself in near darkness. The parachute harness, caught in the door, yanked him to a sudden stop and he fell on his face onto the metal floor.

Right behind him, something hit the metal door. The thunderous clap was deafening. CJ's ears and chest screamed. He expected he'd suffered some permanent hearing loss.

"Are you okay?" Travis asked through now scratchy speakers.

"Awesoman's pounding on the box. Won't keep him out for long."

"Won't need to."

CJ released the harness holding him in the pack, but couldn't move because the heavy machine pinned him to the ground. He wiggled to the side, scraping some of the TM logo off his t-shirt onto the rivets on the floor. He tried to use the pack to help him stand, only to yank his burned fingers back. "Ouch! It's hot!"

"He he. Yeah, that happens when you burn rocket fuel." Travis was still laughing when CJ finally stood and looked out through the small rectangular portal TM had left in the heavy door for light and air.

A few bees from the swarm outside flew in through the small opening. CJ avoided them, still finding it hard to believe they were Awesoman's weakness. When he peeked out, he could see the blue and gold Super flailing his arms around. Even with the ringing in his ears, he heard the man cry out. "Ahh! Get away! Ow!"

Awesoman jumped to fly away, but fell to the ground. He rolled himself up into a ball, using his cape as a kind of tent shield. CJ said into the helmet, "It worked. He's down."

"Great!" CJ could hear the sheer ecstasy in TM's voice. He loved nothing more than when a plan worked. "I'll have my people there to pick him up in one minute. There's a release inside the door. You can get out now."

"Are you kidding?" CJ asked. "There are bees all over the place out there."

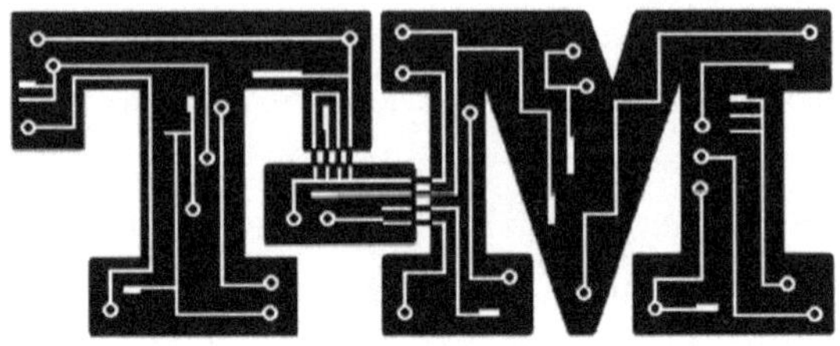

25

CJ watched the news on one of Tech-Monger's laptops as he lay in bed. Despite having what seemed to be unlimited resources, TM didn't care much for the creature comforts. CJ's twin bed was hard and lumpy. It sat in the corner of a storage room with stacks of boxes of all sizes, most of which had various pieces of electrical equipment stacked on them. There were two empty boxes nearby for laundry and a large screen mounted on the wall covered most of the small window. CJ didn't care for the accommodations, but he'd seen Travis's room, and it looked just the same. The kitchen didn't look much different. Crates of soda pop, granola bars, chips, and other junk foods sat around the room with the tops torn off one or more of the boxes of each type, though they remained fastened to the palette with cellophane.

The news, local and national, was having a field day. There wasn't a living soul on the planet who didn't know Awesoman's weakness now. TM made sure the jetpack and protective vault were gone long before the news arrived. Though Awesoman told everybody he'd chased Tech-Monger here, and people all over the city corroborated the story about a flying robot suit, the news focused repeatedly on how the Super had been taken out by a couple of bee stings. Apparently, they were as shocked by the idea as CJ.

"How are you planning to deal with the problem now?" the reporter asked.

Awesoman still had his suit on, but his face was puffy as he responded. "I didn't know about this allergy before. The flying device obviously upset a local hive, but I have people working on a bee-sting proof suit. I'll be back in action soon."

"What about Tech-Monger? How are you planning to deal with him?"

"In light of recent events, the Control Crew will be sending five of their top heroes. The world will be rid of Tech-Monger soon. We have geniuses far in excess of anything this amateur can imagine. It won't take us long to bring him to justice."

CJ shook his head. Things were unfolding exactly as Travis predicted. He couldn't decide if that comforted or worried him.

Standing next to TM, CJ pointed at a Korean woman in a pink and red dress. She was one of the Supers in an online picture of the Control Crew. "That's Harmony Song, martial arts and swordplay master." The news had identified five of the Super team's members as the ones heading to Denver. "She can channel various animal powers. Next to her is Beetle Bomb." He slid his finger to a black-clad muscle man with an iridescent sheen and metallic beetle logo. "He can't be hurt by impact forces and he can see in the dark."

"He sees infrared?"

"I think so. Most of the information we have is from second hand observation. So the gurus on the Internet are sifting between slander from their opponents and gushing fan-boys who claim to have seen them in action. Everybody agrees Vicky Vixen has some kind of mind reading and mind-control powers. You're going to want to watch out for her especially." CJ pointed to a smiling blonde woman with a low-cut outfit and unnaturally white teeth.

"But she doesn't have any Super strength or toughness, right? So regular bullets and such will probably do the job. I just don't let her get close." TM shifted from one foot to the other, uncomfortably.

"Next is Enigma'am. You'll probably never see her at all. She tends to work behind the scenes doing the genius mystic thing. If she ever does make an appearance, she wears this black masquerade mask and a black cloak over a black dress."

Travis wiggled his fingers. "Oooooo."

"Last is Cyberknight." CJ pointed to a knight in shining armor. "He's got tech stuff going on, like you. But he's also a fast and powerful fighter. Rumor has it he's some kind of cyborg, because his armor seems to change what it can do all the time."

"Is he a hacker? Is he weak to being hacked?"

"I don't know." CJ turned in his chair and scratched his head. "There aren't any stories about it listed online."

"So that's it?" TM took the mouse and zoomed in on the picture. "Not the rest of them?"

CJ shrugged. "Five is a lot, actually. Awesoman must suspect more than he's letting on. They usually only send a few for local issues like this. The only time they all show up is when the whole world is in danger. That's only happened three times in the last ten years."

TM moved in closer, studying the picture of Enigma'am. "So they have a genius, a tech guy, a couple of hitters, and a mentalist. That's a pretty targeted response group."

"That's how they do it. Just be glad they didn't send Indom. That guy is completely invulnerable. He literally can't be stopped or hurt."

"Couldn't." Travis stood back and smiled, patting CJ on the back. "He couldn't be stopped. But before now, nobody had you."

"Hover-bikes? Are you kidding me?" TM pointed accusatorily at the news.

CJ watched Vicky Vixen fly past the camera with a determined yet still alluring smile. She was intensively attractive. He wondered if that was one of her powers. "Cyberknight's invention, although most people think Enigma'am had a hand in it, too. People have been trying to get them to release the technology for years, but the Control Crew refuses."

"It's not better than a jetpack, but I must get my hands on one. I have to figure out that anti-grav system. Do you know what I could do with anti-grav tech?" TM's eyebrows knit low.

CJ smiled. He was pretty sure keeping people like Tech-Monger from using it was the exact reason the Control Crew kept their information secret from the public. "I think this time a jetpack would be a bad idea. I'd do better on a building, hidden. Maybe a drone could lure them to me without them knowing."

"You're used to working in the shadows."

"It's kept me alive a long time."

"Okay, we'll make another drone to look like the rocket suit."

CJ TUCKED HIMSELF INTO A CORNER ON THE TOP OF THE FOUR SEASONS HOTEL. What looked like a small decorative detail on the roof from the ground was actually another two-story structure on top of the city's highest building. It had taken him longer than TM wanted just to get up here. TM said through the Bluetooth earpiece, "You should have just flown up there with the jet-pack."

"That defeats the point of being out of sight," CJ said, reminding his boss of his plan. He shifted the phone to his other ear. They hadn't gone over any kind of payment yet. CJ just hoped his salary wouldn't be all in coins from the recent Mint heist.

"Are you ready now?"

"Yes." CJ would have liked to catch his breath, but the cold wind biting into his skin at this height made him want to get it over with as soon as possible.

"We have to cut contact," TM said. "It's a good bet they can track us by this signal if they catch you."

"Okay." CJ pushed the button to hang up, and jammed his hand back in a pocket. The morning breeze felt like a gale so high up.

From his vantage, CJ could see most of the city to the south and east of him. He didn't like the tall pointed steeple on the structure behind him. He thought it might divert the flying Supers away from the building.

Another robot shaped drone lifted into the sky. Travis kept making everything look like smaller versions of the giant exo-suit. CJ figured it was easier for the Supers to identify them as Tech-Monger's work, like villainous branding.

The jet packs on the drone shot the smaller robot forward. They'd identified a few old and useless buildings where nobody would be in the morning. The robot zeroed in on them and launched missiles.

If humans had done it, the NSA would call it terrorism and send out a response team. Since Travis was a Super, they left it to the heroes. CJ had to remind himself, he was a Super now. He was part of this world. He'd never be normal again.

The Control Crew came into view. Well timed and in a wide diamond formation, they rose into the sky a few blocks east of the rampaging bait robot.

CJ's headphone came on. "I hacked their coms. You're welcome." Travis's voice faded and CJ could hear everything the Control Crew said.

"Be ready to scramble on my mark," came an electronically synthesized voice. Cyberknight, whose body flew under its own power, led the way with his sword out and pointed forward. Beetle Bomb and Harmony Song flanked him on either side with flying motorbikes. Vicky Vixen's bike flew behind the others.

"I'm not going to be much help up here," Vicky said in a voice that made CJ's heart speed up. How could just her voice be so alluring?

"No," Enigma'am said. She had a low voice for a woman. "Hold back for now. We'll want you up there when we find Tech-Monger." CJ knew he had to figure out where Enigma'am was as soon as possible. She had a way of turning up at the critical moment in the worst places, for the people the Control Crew fought.

The robot did a tight loop, moving to attack position. The steel body plates glistened in the sunlight. TM's voice boomed from an amplified speaker in the robot's chest. "Four against one. That hardly seems fair. Time to even the odds!"

The left-hand machine gun opened up, spraying randomly in the direction of the approaching team.

Three small missiles blasted from the robot's pack, zeroing in on the front three Supers.

"Scatter." Cyberknight's voice was emotionless. Harmony and Beetle turned away to each side. Vicky hit the brakes, putting more distance between herself and the targets.

Cyberknight flew straight for the missile, swinging his sword in a quick arc.

The explosion diverted to one side as the tip of the sword detonated the device, and his metal plated body flew to the other side. Once the fire cleared and fell to the ground, the knight was still flying toward the robot.

Beetle dipped, catching the missile in the back.

He shrugged it off and veered back toward the fight.

Harmony Song tossed something behind her, probably a throwing star. She was gone when it impacted.

CJ shook his head. This was like morning warm-ups for the Control Crew. Tech-Monger knew as much. The only purpose had been to spread out the team, so they weren't in a tight bunch.

The robot turned and opened the jets up, flying straight for CJ with Cyberknight hot in pursuit. The metal crusader's red cape shook violently in the turbulent air as jets from his metal boots propelled him after the steel bait.

The drone flew right above CJ, turning slightly once past the Four Seasons building. It was a perfect maneuver. Cyberknight followed equally close. CJ could read him. His brain actually connected to the robot body. Cyberknight's weakness was something he took medicine for constantly. Because of the metal interfaces, he needed blood thinners to avoid a heart attack. That wouldn't be something they could exploit easily.

"Mark," Cyberknight said into the com.

Beetle and Harmony flew by next on their air cycles. CJ felt shivers as they went by. "Confirmed," Harmony said. CJ got a reading on each of them.

Vicky, now trailing, went wide on the other side of the building, too far for CJ to get any kind of information about her.

"This thing has no communication line," Cyberknight said. "We can't use it to trace Tech-Monger."

CJ leaned around the corner. When Cyberknight caught up to the robot, it turned and opened fire. Cyberknight weaved to one side, then swiped with his sword two-handed. CJ expected the weapon to bounce off the metal plates, but the precision swing put the blade right into the heart of the bot. The lights inside its beak-like face went out. The jets cut, and the metal husk fell. Beetle, next to arrive, went low and shot a grappling hook around the inanimate drone.

He guided it to land on a building, keeping onlookers below safe from falling debris.

CJ smiled. They were pros.

"Game over." He heard the woman's voice both through the earphone and his free ear. CJ turned around to see a woman with a black masquerade mask in a Gothic black dress and lace cape. She had a dark gray emblem showing the moon phases around the crossed CC logo on her chest.

"Enigma'am," he said, putting up his hands. "How did you get up here?"

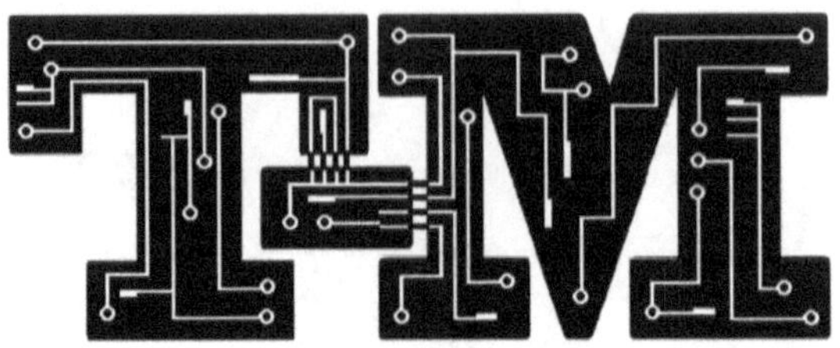

26

Enigma'am reached a hand forward. CJ stepped back from the protection of the wall by him. The wind gusted around the side of the building.

"This isn't what it looks like," CJ said. "I'm not Tech-Monger." He moved to block her hand, unsure if she was going to push him or grab him. He could read her powers and weakness. He knew she had the power to teleport, which is how she'd gotten here so quickly after the others spotted him. Her weakness was meteoric rock. The rest of the team were talking about him when they said, "Mark," and, "Confirm," on their coms. That's how she found him.

She opened her eyes wide, staring into his. Time seemed to slow down. He felt his mind slipping down a water-slide, plunging into deep darkness.

When he snapped out of it. She had his Bluetooth earphone in one black lace gloved hand, and his cell phone in the other. "I got it," she said. Her voice came through the small speaker, too. "They're hacking our coms, just as you predicted."

CJ jumped forward, grabbing his phone.

She dropped the earpiece and disappeared.

"Already traced the hack," Cyberknight said as CJ lifted the device to his ear.

"I'll take the henchman," Harmony said.

"Beetle and Vicky, follow me to the warehouse lair. Cutting coms." Cyberknight turned to the northwest as the line went dead. One of the motorcycles broke from the group and headed back toward CJ. He knew Harmony's powers were enhanced martial arts, toughness, and powerful attacks. He'd never take her in a fight. Her weakness wouldn't help him, either. She would lose her powers if exposed to all four of the arcane magical elements at the same time: fire, water, earth, and air. He couldn't get any of them but air up here.

CJ grabbed the door handle and pulled. The jetpack waited at the top of the stairs. He stepped over the closest wing when Travis started talking in his ear. "We're being monitored. How successful were you?"

CJ didn't want to say, "four out of five," because the Control Crew might figure out what he meant. He said, "Eighty percent." What was the point? They had a genius and a computer on their side. They'd figure it out eventually.

"Take the jetpack," Tech-Monger said. "You don't want to be caught in the building with Harmony."

CJ ran back up the stairs and strapped in. As much as he hated the idea of flying around with all of them out there, he had no chance of escaping their Korean Martial Artist. She could probably jump stairs by flights.

He started the engines and cranked the controls forward before his feet were even in the harness. The noise almost deafened him. The vibrations pained his heart. Smoke filled the stairwell. He choked, held his breath, and blasted out the door. A hover-bike, a few feet from the building's edge, toppled as his robot-shaped pack propelled him past.

Harmony, dressed in a white uniform, grabbed the controls as the vehicle twisted upside-down. Once the anti-gravity lifters flipped, they joined gravity to accelerate the cycle toward the ground.

CJ's feet dangled down at the waist. The steering fins at the back flipped around in the wind, causing the pack to lurch in random directions. Halfway through a loop, the thing twisted. CJ's feet fell back of their own accord. He bent his knees and slid one foot into place before the pack rolled again.

The chemical engines left a long trail behind him as he followed Harmony straight toward the ground.

She managed to do some kind of flip, landing in the seat upside down and righting her machine.

CJ pushed back with his one leg and came out of the dive. He steered away from Harmony, forcing his second foot into the control harness. She was already in pursuit when he straightened up and rammed the throttle full forward again.

She stayed right behind him, a little above and to one side to avoid the black pollution his jetpack emitted. She wasn't gaining on him, but he didn't have much of a lead. If he turned, she'd angle faster and get closer.

"In pursuit on your six." Harmony broke the communication silence.

Ahead, the rest of the Control Crew rose into the air. He'd accidently gone straight toward the warehouse where they were headed to catch Tech-Monger. CJ shook his head. He should have gone the other direction. To what end? He doubted this jetpack had more fuel than the hover-bike chasing him.

CJ slowed as they approached, turning so he levitated in a standing position. He rotated in the direction of Harmony Song. She stayed back, waiting for the rest of the Crew to surround him on four sides.

"Surrender," Cyberknight said through the phone link. "We know you weren't directly responsible for the murders. If you come peacefully, we have the authority to guarantee you won't get the death penalty like Tech-Monger."

CJ gently maneuvered his pack closer to Vicky, hoping to get closer to her while he tried to figure out what to do. None of the Supers had any weaknesses he could exploit. Vicky Vixen hovered her bike away from him.

He stopped and stayed in place.

She'd been the weakest fighter on a Super team for too long. Everybody they faced would try to go through her first. The others would expect it.

"I'm not part of this," CJ said. "I don't want to fight any of you."

"Then land your mini-jet and surrender," Cyberknight said. His synthesized voice held no judgment. "If you're innocent, the judge will let you off."

CJ knew no judge in the world would let him go. His on-board computer had missiles locked on each of the four Supers hovering around him. With the touch of a button, he could try fighting his way out. Would he bet his life on Tech-Monger's jetpack over Cyberknight's flying cycles?

These guys were pros. They wouldn't still be here if they went down every time somebody shot a missile at them. If they destroyed his pack, he'd probably die. Death or life in prison? He'd never contemplated which fate he wanted less.

He eased back on the thruster, slowly lowering toward the ground. If he offered to change sides and join them, would they take him seriously? The only thing he had to offer was his power to help them. He'd have to tell them what he could do, and then Tech-Monger's weakness.

He shook his head and kept descending. He'd bet money Travis had some kind of override destruct button on this jetpack. As soon as he started talking, he'd probably be turned into a burning ball of rocket fuel. A new fear gripped him. If the Control Crew got close enough, would Tech-Monger blow him up to get to them?

When CJ hovered less than a hundred feet above the ground, he saw the Tech-Monger's titanic exo-suit rise from the ground. Making enough noise to be heard above CJ's pack, it rose as high as one of the downtown sky-scrapers. The monster raised one arm toward the group.

CJ jammed the throttle and turned toward Vicky. His jetpack shot forward as a cone of fire filled the area.

The Control Crew scattered. Some of the flames caught Cyberknight as he dropped below the torrent, singeing his cape. Vicky spun her cycle and sped toward the back of Tech-Monger. She reacted too late, CJ managed to get near enough to read her powers and weakness before she went a different direction. Acetone vapor? He didn't even know what that was. How could he read a weakness he didn't even understand?

Just getting that close, CJ wanted to beg her forgiveness. Even knowing she charmed people, he felt a powerful infatuation for her. He turned the pack so he could hover and watch the action.

Smaller, more traditional drones with propellers at each corner, rose up around Tech-Monger. One began to follow each of the Control Crew from high up. Others started making quick sniping runs, weaving until they were in position and then firing a single shot at the flying Supers. Harmony and Vicky dodged the little pests, Beetle and Cyberknight ignored the ping of bullets.

Two of the cycles charged. Tech-Monger twisted his arm and opened up with machine gun fire, forcing Harmony and Beetle to break off their attack and double back.

A hatch opened in the back of the colossal machine. The great device swiveled, grabbing CJ's jetpack out of the sky with its claw. Then the arm twisted at unnatural angles and deposited the whole flying machine in the back of its torso. Before closing the portal.

Vicky tried to follow CJ in, only to turn off at the last minute when the huge arm swatted at her like a bug.

CJ killed the engines and released the harness, pulling his legs free of the steering fins. He clutched one arm to his chest. Why hadn't he just kept going? With the Control Crew and Tech-Monger fighting each other, he had a perfect chance to get away. Now he was back in the belly of the beast. Despite the size difference, he didn't like Tech-Monger's odds in this fight.

The big robot began to move with a lurch. CJ fell on his butt, sliding around until he could get to the sidewall and grab a rail fastened there. He couldn't see or hear what was going on outside except Travis's voice coming through giant speakers mounted in the behemoth.

"Now you will face the full power of my exo-armor!"

Muffled explosions echoed as the massive hydraulics stomped through buildings and cars.

CJ pulled himself up and pushed the elevator button. He concentrated on keeping his balance. Stairs would have been impossible to climb with the whole robot torso jumping around erratically, even if he could catch his breath.

CJ pulled the Bluetooth earpiece out and dialed with his phone.

Juliet answered. "Hello?"

"It's dad."

"What's going on? Are you in that big robot thing again? The news says the Control Crew is…"

"I know." CJ spoke loud to be heard over all the noise. "Listen, are you at home? You have to get to safety. I think this thing is heading in your direction. It'll crush a whole building with one step."

"Mom's not home."

"You need to not be home either. Don't take anything. Just go now. Run!"

Juliet yelled into the phone, but something hit the metal wall on the outside next to him and it echoed through the whole room like a drum. Had one of the cycles crashed into TM's robot?

The elevator door opened. He went in. "Get somewhere safe!"

"Where?" Juliet's voice wasn't sobbing or scared. She seemed resolved and he couldn't be prouder.

"The church. Stay with Father Weaver."

"Okay." He heard some commotion on her end of the line. "I love you, daddy."

"Be safe. I love…" The line went dead.

He pushed the button on the wall, then sat on the floor of the elevator as it rose. Holding firm to the handrail, he wondered how this much movement didn't tear the elevator apart. He tried her again. No answer.

He dialed Delia's number. It went to a message. As soon as it beeped he said, "Delia, big things are going down. Bad things. Get somewhere safe. I'm sorry for everything."

When the doors opened again, he stumbled past TM's gyroscopic control platform and strapped into the chair.

"You made it!" Travis had a big dumb grin on his face beneath the virtual reality visor covering his eyes. He jumped and twisted as he pushed the huge robot to its limit. "Tell me you have something we can use against these guys. Another couple hits and I think we're done for."

With his limited view through the airplane windshield, CJ saw a cycle zip past them. Six missiles launched, splitting in three directions and bending out of sight. The explosions were quiet, and jostled the huge moving fortress.

"Sorry," CJ said. He made sure his phone was off. "I got a read on four of them, but it's nothing we can exploit from up here. Beetle's weakness is his stomach, but he keeps it wrapped in Kevlar."

"Okay." Travis stopped, clenched his teeth, then reached out an arm. The room rattled as machine gun fire lanced out into the city. To CJ's horror, he realized Travis wasn't worried about collateral damage. The bullets shattered windows, cut into cars, and blasted through concrete walls, consigning any people in the path to a fate based on whether they were lucky enough to be missed.

Then the marching robot stopped. "Freeze!" he said through the big speakers. Travis turned his left arm to the side and twisted his body. "One more move, and everybody in that building dies."

As the robot followed TM's movement, CJ could see the building being held hostage. Beneath them stood the steeple and stained-glass windows of the Church of Saint Augustine.

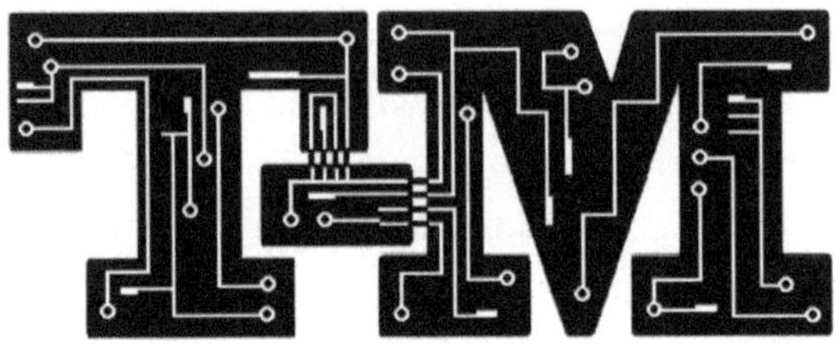

27

An eerie silence crept in where the sounds of explosions and roaring engines nearly deafened them before. From inside the spinning gyroscopes, Travis said, "Lift your feet."

CJ didn't remember obeying, but he must have because one second later the ground sizzled with electric current. When Enigma'am appeared out of thin air, she screeched and fell over.

"Ha ha!" Travis held his pose threatening the church, but the whole top of the robot shook back and forth as he wagged his head. "I knew she'd try that. Can't have her talking to me, now, can I."

CJ made sure the Super was still breathing despite convulsing in a fetal position. He kept his feet up even after the buzzing died down.

"I need you to connect me to the local television stations," TM said next.

"What? How?" CJ pulled his gaze toward the control panel. He felt numb. Outside he saw three of the control crew hovering on the other side of the building. "I don't see Beetle Bomb out there."

"Your tip paid off. I used his weakness against him. I caught him around the middle with the claw and crushed him. Kevlar can't stop three-thousand-pound hydraulics! Now find the switches labeled 'transmit,' and flip them to the upward position."

CJ complied. Tech-Monger had crushed, maybe killed Beetle Bomb. That was CJ's fault. All his life, he'd stayed out of the business of Supers, living the life of a normal on the periphery. Now he was an accessory to murder. How many murders? He was a fugitive from the law. A Supervillain had missiles pointed at his daughter, the only human being on the planet who still thought well of him. He was in a machine that was threatening to kill his priest. Sure, CJ was excommunicated, but that didn't change all the years Father Weaver had listened to his confessions and given him advice. Why hadn't CJ taken it? What was he trying to prove?

CJ felt bile rise in his throat as Tech-Monger bellowed through the big speakers. "Control Crew, Denverites, and people everywhere, I am the Tech-Monger. I don't want to kill anybody. I can help the world be a better place. I refuse to be arrested because these so-called heroes antagonized me. If you don't back away, I will begin making a huge mess!"

CJ shook his head. TM's words didn't even make any sense. Was Travis crazy? With his big smile and frequent giggle-laughs, he looked it.

Enigma'am was out cold.

CJ quietly pushed the button on the belts holding him in place. His whole life, he'd been fooling himself. He tried to pretend the actions of Supers had nothing to do with him. Everybody else saw it. They knew what made people heroes and villains. CJ always insisted what mattered was being a Super or a normal. Now he realized that didn't matter at all. The only important thing was the thing he never let himself think about or accept. The only thing that mattered was whether somebody was a hero or a villain.

Travis was a villain. Maybe Jakak had been motivated by a real desire to change things for the better. Farseer definitely wasn't out to hurt anybody. But Tech-Monger was a villain, evil to the core. He killed without a thought. He obviously didn't think this all through, or they wouldn't be holding hostages in a standoff with some of the world's greatest Supers.

No, not just Supers, heroes. Whatever their faults, they tried to protect people and make the world better. If they couldn't stop Tech-Monger, CJ had to try. Unfortunately, their best hope lay at his feet. If Enigma'am had just spoken, maybe one word, Travis's weakness would have brought this all to an end.

"You need to stop," CJ said.

"What?" Travis turned his head, causing the whole robot to twist before he remembered the VR controls and faced back toward the church. CJ fell out of his seat. "Are you kidding? We can't stop now."

"What's your escape plan?" CJ stood, rubbing his chest. "This thing is huge. We'll never manage to get away now that we're on the news and the Control Crew is following us."

"You think so little of me?" Travis scoffed. "Show some faith, man."

CJ couldn't trust TM. All he wanted was to get Juliet out of danger. "You have a plan?"

"Of course. There's a rocket in the body of this exo-suit. If things go wrong, we'll just blast off into space."

"Space? They can find you in orbit, I'm sure."

"But not the landing pod. It's too small to show up on radar. We'll disappear and regroup until we're ready for round two."

Cyberknight's voice came through the com channel. "We're moving back, Tech-Monger. Don't hurt any more innocent people."

"See! We've brought the Control Crew to their knees!" Travis did a little leap, causing the whole machine to shake up and down. CJ fell to the ground again. Enigma'am moaned and then went unconscious again. He looked at the many tools and gadgets fastened all over in the cockpit room.

"My daughter's in that church," CJ said as he stood again. "Please, don't hurt her. She's the only thing I have left in the world."

Travis tipped his head to the side, tossing CJ into the chair face first. "I'm sorry, man. I wish I'd known. I could have picked a different building. But now? I can't afford to reposition this machine. Hopefully things won't go bad."

"Hopefully?" CJ slumped in the chair. His chest hurt, but not from the bullet wound. His heart ached.

"We're in a standoff," Tech-Monger said. "They will try and wait it out. I really wish I hadn't used this virtual reality control system. I'm going to get tired of this pose soon."

"What if we just attacked the Control Crew instead?" CJ had given up on trying to live through this ordeal. He just wanted Juliet safe.

"That's pointless." TM laughed, shaking the room. "There will always be more heroes out there. The only way is to show them they can't beat me."

CJ didn't bother explaining how more would always come. Beating these five would just draw out an army of heroes. His phone vibrated in his pocket. Since TM was busy, he pulled it out. Delia.

CJ walked back toward the elevator. "I left something in the jetpack. I'll be back."

As soon as the door closed, he accepted the call. "Hello?"

"CJ?"

"I'm so glad you called me. I just want to say that I'm sorry for everything. All these years I…"

"Not now!" He stopped and tipped his head to the side. She went on, "That big machine is about to kill me."

"You're in the church, too?"

"Obviously."

CJ's head spun. "What are you doing there?"

"I was here talking to Father Weaver when Juliet ran in and said your monster machine was taking over the city."

"It's not mine. It's Tech-Monger's. I'm just…"

"His thug, yes, I get it. But I'm afraid. How can you sit by and watch him kill your daughter?"

"I'm not," CJ said. "I'm trying to stop him."

"How? Because so far he doesn't look like he's going to stop."

"I'm working on it, I…"

Father Weaver's voice broke in. "CJ?"

"I'm here, Father."

"You've fallen so far. You're supposed to rise above the lot life gives you. Why did you join the villains as soon as you got your powers?"

"It was a mistake. I know that now. I'm getting out of the villain business for good."

"You didn't correct me for calling them villains."

CJ wiped the sweat from his forehead. "No. I finally understand."

"Then what are you going to do about it?"

"I'm going to be a hero. Now put Delia back on." The elevator lurched. CJ needed to know what was happening out there.

"Hello?"

"I love you, Delia. I just need you to know that. I can't think of any way for this to end well. But I finally understand."

"I..." The line went dead. CJ held up the phone. Out of battery. He punched the elevator button. As the doors opened, Enigma'am stood up, only to be shocked again and fall back down. When the crackling died down, CJ stepped forward cautiously.

Through the front window, behind the Control Crew, a dozen fighter jets raced toward them.

"About time. I need you to send the drones after those fighter ships." CJ knew what happened next. Travis wouldn't let anybody else win, ever. The government and the Supers would escalate it until Travis killed everybody CJ loved. CJ walked over to one of the framing bars and pulled the two latches holding a crowbar in place. He caught it as it fell.

Thou shalt not kill.

CJ shook his head. He'd do whatever it took to protect the people he cared about.

Travis, concentrating on the incoming jets, lifted the hand not threatening the church and began firing the machine gun.

CJ swung the red crowbar as hard as he could. The outer gyroscope ring on TM's control platform broke, flipping pieces off into the room. The motor whined as the two other rings began to compensate.

CJ smacked the next one.

Travis jerked back to look at CJ as the gyroscopes disintegrated. The whole machine lurched, sending CJ flying. He caught the chair and landed hard.

Still controlling the vessel but from an unstable platform, Tech-Monger moved carefully to keep from throwing himself to the ground.

"After everything I've done for you, this is how you repay me?"

"This is wrong," CJ said. "I can't let you destroy that church."

"Try and stop me!" Tech-Monger turned back toward the old brick building with stained glass glistening in the morning sun.

CJ jumped up, then back as the electric floor began to buzz. He felt a sting in his toe, but luckily escaped Enigma'am's fate. She just shook in place as the ground sizzled.

Travis raised his hand. CJ could see the missiles aligning to their target. It would only take one, but Tech-Monger would unleash many to make his point.

CJ jumped from the chair.

As TM pulled the trigger in his control glove, CJ brought the crowbar down on the wire-rigged arm.

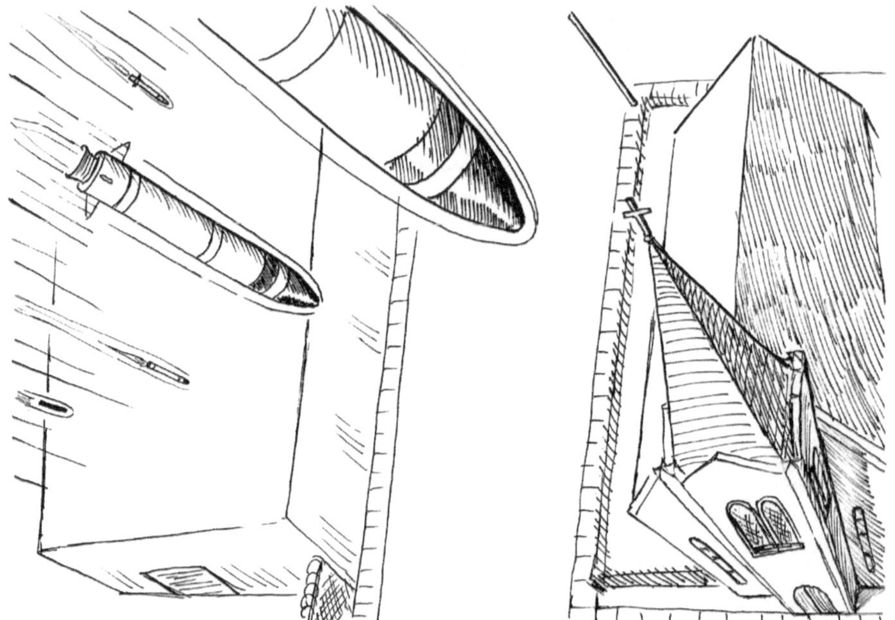

"Aah!" TM's arm shattered and dropped. The robot lurched down as Travis screamed. The missiles launched, exploding in turns until nothing but fire and smoke filled the view through the front windshield.

"Nooooooo!" CJ screamed at the windshield as if he could turn back time by yelling.

Through gritted teeth, Tech-Monger said, "I'd have thought you'd learned by now. Nobody beats me."

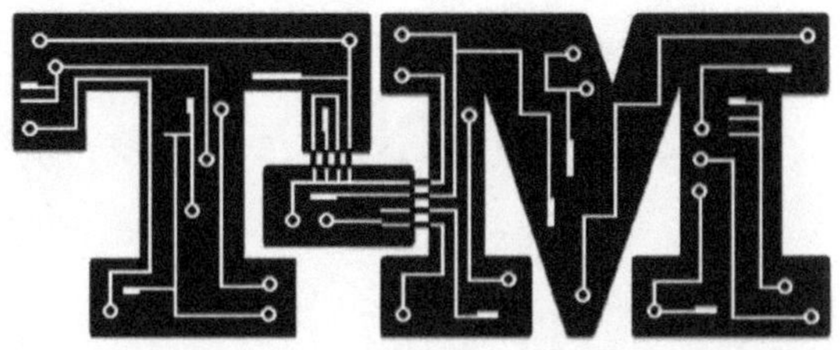

28

obody beats you?" CJ asked. Sweat poured down his face as the temperature in the converted cockpit rose drastically from the nearby fire of the destroyed church. The churning lights cast garish shadows against the back wall and elevator door. Ash streaked the front window. The electrical floor stopped buzzing.

"No," Tech-Monger said, clutching his arm across the front of his body. Still connected to the exo-suit controls, the giant thing outside had its weapon arms crossed, too.

"Think again," CJ said. "You killed everybody I loved. So now, I'm going to *beat you*—to death."

He lifted up the crowbar and brought it down.

Half the time, CJ brought the metal bar down on the electronic control panels near the windshield. The other half, he hit Tech-Monger.

"Oof."

"Aaarh!"

Whenever he hit Tech-Monger, the machine fell closer to the ground until Travis lay screaming on the floor. All the wires connected to his arms and legs splayed across the pad, severed and frayed.

The windshield shattered as the machine died, letting black smoke fill the room. The temperature rose until it woke Enigma'am, who sat up and coughed. CJ, choking, kicked Tech-Monger's face so the man was looking up at him. CJ held the crowbar like a sword, the wedge end pointing at the fallen villain's nose.

"I was wrong about you," CJ said. "Your powers might be weak to women, but your real weakness is stupidity."

He walked over to Enigma'am and helped her up. "I'm sorry I couldn't get to you sooner. I don't think there's any way out of here."

She shook her head, coughed, and grabbed his bicep.

The world around him disappeared.

CJ FELT THE SUN AND A COOL BREEZE ON HIS SWEATY FACE. ENIGMA'AM ALMOST fell over, so he caught her. "Teleporting is a great power," he said, as if she didn't already know.

"Thanks," she huffed, letting go of his arm and stabilizing herself. Into her com she said, "Tech-Monger is still alive inside, but he won't last long."

The fire raged a dozen yards away, blocking most of their view of the titanic metal machine. All of TM's drones had fallen out of the sky when CJ destroyed the controls, so the remaining members of the Control Crew rushed forward to pull him out of the fiery mess. The fighter jets flew past the scene, doubling back in case they might still be needed.

The church still stood! The missiles had exploded in front of it because CJ diverted their path down when he hit Travis's arm. From the high up fuselage, he couldn't see past the fire and smoke. CJ raised his arms and said a prayer of thanks as he began to limp toward it.

The doors opened and a dozen people came out. Juliet and Father Weaver turned with most of the crowd to look at the huge fire as the Control Crew bravely cut their way in and saved Tech-Monger.

Delia broke from the group and ran toward CJ. She threw her arms around him and crushed him to her. The pain in his chest didn't bother him much at all. Her tears mingled with his sweat. She kissed his forehead, then his lips.

CJ concentrated on standing up and enjoying the moment.

"I knew you were a hero after all," she said. "I knew it."

"Thanks for believing in me." He kissed her back. "But it's not going to last long."

"What? Why?" She flipped a lock of red hair out of her way, so she could stare into his eyes when he answered.

"I'm a wanted man. An escaped convict. They're going to put me in jail for the rest of my life."

"Even after you did all this?" She pointed with one hand.

"I don't think they will see it that way."

Juliet came next. She jumped between the two of them, wrapping her arms around CJ's waist. "You made it. I thought you were going to die."

"I made it," he said, moving his hands from Delia to his daughter. "But I was more worried about you. Weren't you afraid?"

"Not for a minute." Juliet stepped back and looked in his face. "I knew you'd save me from the very first."

A wave of heat blasted past them as something on Tech-Monger's exo-suit exploded. CJ hoped the Control Crew were all safe. He took a deep breath. "I don't deserve a daughter as good as you."

"That's true," she said.

Father Weaver approached next. CJ reached his hand out to shake, but found himself caught in another hug. The priest said, "Well done."

"I'm just glad you're all okay. And the church, of course."

"It was a miracle," Father Weaver said.

"A miracle and this." CJ lifted the crowbar up. Why hadn't he put it down?

They all laughed. Delia said, "You are the miracle today."

"I'm a Super now," CJ said. "I realized I had to make a choice. Any chance I can use that to appeal my excommunication? I mean, I'm probably going to jail for the rest of my life, but it would be nice to have something to look forward to after I die."

Delia and Juliet both tucked under one of his arms to look at Father Weaver with their big, doe eyes.

"I hadn't actually gotten around to mailing in the paperwork," the priest admitted. "I think in light of this new change, I can probably suspend it. You can't work for any more Supervillains, though."

"I swear." CJ raised his hand above Juliet's shoulder.

"I can't do anything about the police, though," Father Weaver said.

Delia teared up. "It looks like I lose you no matter what."

CJ pulled her closer as Father Weaver turned to inspect the damage to the church's parking lot. Juliet's phone rang. She ducked out from under CJ's arm and plugged her other ear.

"Hello? Mom! No, no. Don't worry. I'm fine... We were in the church, but it didn't blow up. Dad saved me. He saved all of us... Yes... No... No, really, he was amazing." She looked up and beamed a smile at her father.

CJ waved as she turned and walked away, still talking. For the first time in a long time he felt like he'd set a good example for his daughter.

"Honestly, Mom, he was the hero of the day. The Control Crew showed up to fight Tech-Monger's giant robot, but he threatened to blow up the church…"

Delia wiped her eyes and looked up. "I'm sorry. It's just been such an emotional day."

As the adrenaline wore off, more and more pain seeped in. CJ began to feel himself slump, letting the crowbar slip until it rested on the ground.

"You must be exhausted," Delia said. "Let's go inside where you can sit down."

She supported him as they went back inside the church. CJ found a wooden pew halfway up and sighed as he deflated. A few pieces of stained glass had broken, letting beams of white light land on the walls. Even bruised and exhausted, having his arm around Delia alone in the church felt good.

"Ask me again," Delia said.

CJ, meditating on the nature of divinity, turned to look at her face. A ray of sunlight lit her from behind like an angel. "Right now, while we wait for the cops to come and arrest me?"

"Right now." She was so beautiful.

CJ twisted sideways off the bench and put one sore knee gingerly on the hard floor. He looked into her eyes. This felt good. A church was the right place. "Delia Thompson, will you marry me?"

"Yes!" She threw her arms around him again and kissed him. CJ stifled a moan and slid back up to the bench. He didn't mind making-out in church, but he knew Father Weaver wouldn't approve. Still, they probably had a good excuse if anybody did.

"Wait," he said.

She tipped her head to the side. "What now?"

"I don't have a ring."

She pulled a little bag out of her pocket and opened it with long, red fingernails. As she tipped it, a small diamond rolled out onto her palm.

"You kept it!" He smiled wide.

"I kept it."

He pulled her into another long kiss. They stopped when the door opened, spreading garish sunlight around the room and making a macabre chiaroscuro behind the crucifix.

"Colin John Leon de la Cruz?" It was a gruff man's voice.

CJ stood up and turned to see two officers. "That's me."

"CJ, you're under arrest."

He kissed Delia on the head once more, pitying her sigh. He handed her the crowbar. "Hold onto this for me?" She sniffed and nodded, taking it out of his hands and clutching it to her like a teddy bear. He stepped to the center aisle and put his wrists out.

They ratcheted the cuffs on. At least they didn't force his hands behind his back. They read him his rights and marched him outside into the bright light where firemen worked on the rest of the fires and a plume of gray smoke rose into the air until it blew away from the church.

Juliet, Delia, and Father Weaver were alive. The church was still standing. CJ took a deep, ashy breath and smiled. Any amount of time in prison would be worth it.

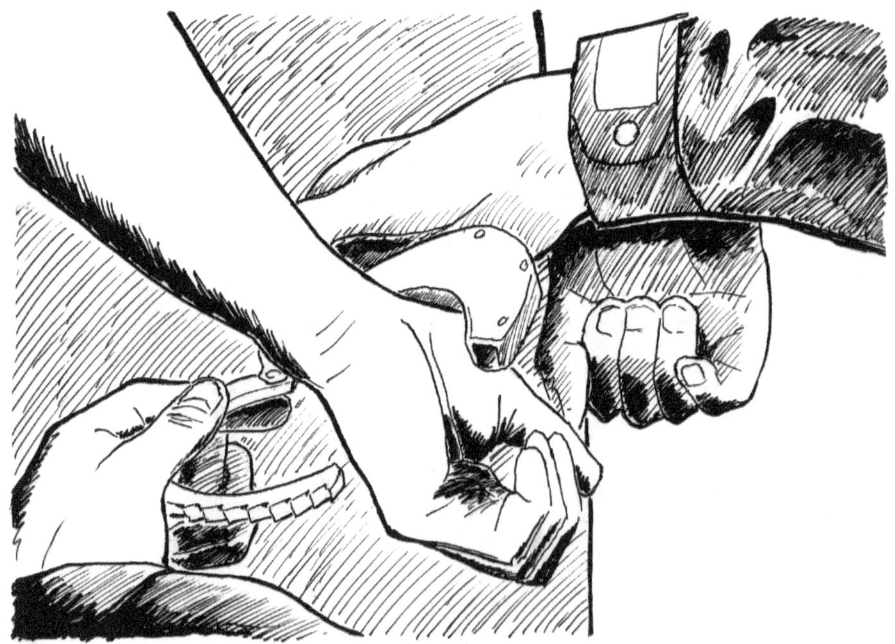

29

CJ looked down at the orange jumpsuit and laughed to himself. If he was out, he'd probably be wearing a Broncos shirt the same color anyway. He had a couple of books sitting on the cot next to him: a graphic novel called *Borderline Boy*, and a book about psychology. Maybe the latter would help him understand his father better. *Thou shalt honor they father and thy mother.* He watched all the news about how the Control Crew showed up in the nick of time to stop the evil Tech-Monger and save a church. Now they were interviewing Harmony Song. She kept her answers short, refusing to editorialize about anything she had not personally seen or done during the battle.

During a commercial, CJ reached up to change the channel when the large, silent guard approached. CJ saw the man pull out his key.

"Somebody wants to talk to me?" CJ asked.

The dark man nodded as the cell creaked open.

CJ followed him down the hall to the interrogation room. He pointed, so CJ went in and sat down. After a few minutes scanning the one-way mirror, CJ heard something strange in the hall.

"Detective Barton?" CJ asked.

Cyberknight walked through the door with his metal boots pounding on the ground. His sword stood sheathed over his back and he pointed with one metal gauntlet at CJ. "I am not Detective Barton."

"Cyberknight!" CJ jumped up and put out a hand, then decided he couldn't really shake a metal gauntlet. "What brings you here?"

"Enigma'am said you took Tech-Monger out on your own at great personal risk." His metallic voice wasn't as annoying as it had been through the Bluetooth earpiece.

"Well, he was a bigger risk to everybody else."

"Enigma'am says you are a Super." Cyberknight's helmet showed no expressions.

"Yes." CJ stepped back. Up close, talking to a robotic suit of armor intimidated him.

"And you can somehow divine a way to defeat any Super?"

CJ thought Enigma'am had been passed out during that part of the conversation. Still, there didn't seem like much reason to deny it now. "Yes."

"Do you know *my* weakness?" Cyberknight leaned forward. Even though his helmet and visor didn't move, CJ could swear the guy was scowling.

CJ leaned back and said quietly, "Yes."

Cyberknight stood up straight again. "We didn't know every Super had a weakness. That's something the Control Crew could put to good use. Plus, you've got the courage to bring down a giant machine from the inside while you're still in it. Enigma'am and I agree you are a good candidate to join our crew. I can't promise anything, but if the rest of the Control Crew agrees to offer you a job, we might be able to get them to commute your prison sentence."

CJ gasped, then smiled. "I thought you only took level four Supers."

Cyberknight shook his helmet. It squeaked. "That's just speculation on the Internet. We take anybody with a heroic heart and skills the team needs."

CJ nodded. "I'd be honored, if they want me."

The metal man nodded once, turned, and clanked out the still-open door.

A FEW DAYS LATER, CJ COULDN'T WAIT FOR DELIA TO FINISH HER NIGHT SHIFT. With the sun smearing orange across the clouds, he texted her to come and meet him out front. When she stepped through the wire-reinforced glass door, he smiled and held up a white gold ring with a big diamond sticking out of the top. She gasped, eyes wide.

"So, how attached are you to working at Lucky Break Bail Bonds?" He tipped his head to indicate the big green neon dollar sign flashing in the widow.

Delia smiled as she let him slide the ring onto her finger. "It's so big!"

She kissed him and gave him a long hug. When it ended, he said, "So?"

"So what? It's amazing! Thank you!"

"Not that. I mean, thanks. But what about your work?"

She tipped her head, letting a lock of red hair fall forward. "What do you mean, how attached am I?"

CJ shrugged. "Well, I mean, these days a lot of women take their career very seriously and I just want to see how you feel about yours."

"I've been working here for ten years. I work with a lot of people I consider to be friends. Is that what you mean?"

"Yes." CJ bit his lip. "It turns out if I want to stay out of jail, I have to work for the Control Crew. They offered me a position on the team."

"Wouldn't you want to anyway?" Her eyes sparkled as she looked at the diamond. The colorful sunset helped. She tipped her head back to him. "You *do* want to be on the Control Crew, right?"

"Of course. The food's way better than in prison to start with. And I guess it pays pretty well. They have sponsors that give them buckets of cash. Supposedly they will give some of that to me, so that's pretty great."

"Then what's the problem?"

"I'll have to move to New York. But I don't want to go if you don't want to go with me."

Delia looked at him and laughed in his face. Then she pulled the glass door open and yelled in, "Hey, boss?"

"Your break's up." The man's voice sounded bored and perturbed at the same time.

"I quit."

"Don't let the door hit you on the way out."

She let it swing shut and smiled. "So tell me more about these buckets of cash."

"Well, some people think it's wrong for Super*heroes* to work for corporate sponsors." It still felt strange for him to say the word. Delia seemed to like it though.

"Whatever." She patted his head. "Buy me a house first. Then we'll worry about the ethics."

"And I'll probably be in danger a lot."

"We'll get life insurance."

"Wouldn't you want to wait and have a big wedding?"

"We'll stop in Vegas before we go."

"You're really mine," he said, staring at her wide open eyes.

"Nope." She grabbed his hand and pulled him away from the Lucky Break. "You're really mine."

"And you just believe I'm a good guy now after all that time?"

She kissed him as they walked. "You were always a good guy. You just didn't know it yet."

"I'll need a Superhero name. They said it shouldn't be anything that gives away my power."

"Well, don't use your e-mail address. I don't think Broncos-Fan-2784 is going to fit on the front of your shirt."

"I'm serious. This is a big decision. Most of the good ones have been taken already. Awesoman, for example."

"Those kinds of names are too self-congratulatory. Can't you pick something a little less obnoxious?"

"Like what?"

"I don't know. Cutie Pie?"

CJ stopped, rolled his eyes, and put out a hand. "Give me the ring back."

"Okay, I'm just kidding. Do you have to decide now?"

"Pretty soon. You need to know what name to change yours to when we're married."

"I thought Cruz. Or Leon De La Cruz."

CJ smiled. "That'll work. No, seriously, if I don't pick something quick somebody else will think of one for me… and that seldom goes well." He thought of the name Mirror Max had given him. Probe-boy. He shuddered. Tech-Monger had unknowingly spared CJ a great deal of ridicule by killing everybody who ever heard that name.

"It can't give away your powers, so not Scanner or Achilles' Heel."

"Right. *Not* those."

Delia snapped her fingers and started walking again. "I've got it! I know the perfect name for you."

CJ's eyes went wide. "What is it?"

She shook her head. "I'm not telling you yet."

"Why not? I did point out that we're in a hurry, right?" All the names he'd come up with so far were awful. Pry Bar? He rolled his eyes.

"I'll tell you after we're married. It will be my wedding present to you."

"Are you serious?"

She stopped smiling. "I am. Dead serious."

CJ studied her face. "You're not kidding."

"Nope. I have the exact right Superhero name for you. I know how important it is, now that you're on the Control Crew. So I want this to be something special I can give you."

"That's great. You're really awesome." CJ scratched his chin. "So, you're really going to just leave me in suspense?"

"You're a Superhero now, CJ. You should probably get used to cliff-hangers."

ABOUT THE AUTHOR

Growing up on a steady diet of Spider-man cartoons and television shows like Batman and Wonder Woman, James Wymore knew he would someday find his own super power and join the fight for justice. He did everything right, from experimenting with arson to jumping from great heights, but his ability to control fire or fly never kicked in.

As he went past the teenage years, he accepted that he probably didn't have a hidden mutant power waiting to manifest. Neither would he uncover any unexplained alien origins, so he threw himself into searching for enhancements designed to bring his latent abilities to the surface. He travelled the world studying arcane magic. Throughout college, he experimented with volatile chemicals, extreme temperatures, lasers, and various forms of radiation.

Eventually, he discovered the power of hypnosis through fantastic stories. He plunged into writing, filling his work with the subtle triggers that would allow him to one day take control of all his readers' minds and use them as an army to conquer the literary world. Until that day, he works tirelessly to create more and better books.

Follow his progress at http://jameswymore.wordpress.com

ABOUT THE ILLUSTRATOR

While most kids put down their crayons and pencils, John Christian Perkins was just getting started. He relished in all things horror, sci-fi and fantasy. He would fill reams of paper with epic dragon battles and *Tales From the Crypt* creatures and mansions. Although he knew little about comic books, he found himself writing and illustrating a satirical comic book series with his friends in high school. Together his group of friends wrote, illustrated, printed and sold copies of their comic book to their classmates, which became a hit! He represented Utah at a national summit of Future Student Leaders in Art in New York City in 2006. He graduated high school as the Sterling Scholar in Art.

He enjoyed expressing his opinion and ruffling some feathers as an award-winning editorial cartoonist for both the *University Journal* at Southern Utah University and for his hometown newspaper, Tooele Utah's *Transcript Bulletin*. He graduated Cumma Sum Laude with a BFA in Studio Arts, emphasis in Illustration. He enjoys adventure, film, history, the great outdoors and long distance running. He dreams of pursuing art full-time. John Christian resides in Georgia with his wife, Vanessa, their daughter, Everest, and dog, Boromir. See more of his work and contact him on his website: www.drawformeJCP.com

This has been an
Immortal Production